CONUNDRUM IN CAPE HOPE

CAPE HOPE MYSTERIES

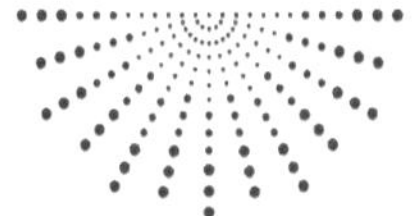

WINNE REED

CONUNDRUM IN CAPE HOPE

CAPE HOPE MYSTERIES BOOK FIVE

Online dating can be murder...

Sylvia Harmon's daughters, Emma and Darcy, have finally convinced her to join the online dating scene. Except that the women in Sylvia's new beau's life seem to have been dropping like flies.

Can Emma keep out of this new mystery?

Join Emma on her next adventure with the adorable Lola, Detective McHottie. Will a certain photographer decide to make an appearance?

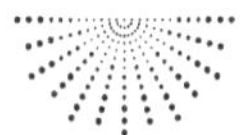

CHAPTER ONE

There were certain situations a daughter never imagined herself living out.

Depending on the circumstances, they became more likely. A sick parent meant she might have to brace herself for the possibility of losing that parent earlier than she'd expected. A divorced parent meant she'd have to get over the idea of them finding somebody new.

I'd already been through that part. Dad and Holly were going strong, and Holly was carrying my baby brother or sister.

Still.

After all the years since my parents' divorce.

It never occurred to me that I'd be sitting in my mom's bedroom, helping her pick out an outfit for her all-important third date with a man she'd met online.

Granted, she had no idea what Darcy or I meant when we snickered about this being the third date. And there I was, thinking we were finally making a reference that wouldn't go completely over her head.

"I don't understand why you think this date is particularly important," Mom sighed, holding up one dress, then another, in front of herself. "We're just going for seafood over at Lou's."

"It's not about what you're actually doing," Darcy reminded her before rolling her eyes my way. "It's about…"

"What you're actually doing," I snickered. She swatted at me.

"I don't understand what you're talking about! Either of you." Mom shook her head. "Both of you. I thought I raised nice girls."

"You did," I insisted, winking at my sister. "And we know you know what we're talking about, or you wouldn't be accusing us of not being nice girls."

"Enough of this talk," she sniffed, turning to face us with a dress held up in front of her. "What do you think about this?"

I wanted to hide my frown, but it wasn't easy. "I think that would look nice covering your sofa." The big, flowery pattern overwhelmed her.

"It makes you look older," Darcy added, wincing when Mom threw a dirty look her way. "I'm sorry, but it's true."

"It's true," I added. "We're not trying to make you feel bad, but you're still a young woman. You should dress more youthfully."

"And your clothes are all from ages ago. When was the last time you went shopping?"

Mom dropped the dress. "Why don't I just find a shovel in the garage and dig myself a grave?"

"Mom…" I sighed.

"No, really. Since I don't deserve to live. I dress like an old lady, my clothes are outdated, and I have no hope of keeping a man interested." Mom sat on the bed with a thud. "I don't know why I'm wasting my time. I can't compete."

"Don't say that!" I threw an arm around her shoulders. "We're only trying to help. Hey, if he weren't interested, there wouldn't be any third date. He obviously likes you."

"You're the one who asked us to come and help you find something nice to wear," Darcy added. "It wouldn't hurt you to shake things up a little."

"I admit," Mom said, exhaling, "I've let things go over the years. Too busy working. I don't think about things like, you know. Updating my wardrobe." She snickered, rolling her eyes.

"You say that like it's a bad thing," I chided. "It isn't. You deserve to take care of yourself, too. Hey, I brought a few things with me, just in case."

"You can't say you let things go when you've been the same size my entire life," Darcy reminded her as I grabbed my tote bag. "I mean, you work around baked goods all day, and you never gain a pound."

"I'm on my feet all the time," Mom pointed out, eyeing the clothes I was pulling out like she expected them to attack her or something.

"You've got it going on," I said, dropping things on the flowered bedspread. She had a thing for floral prints. "You just have to. You know. Not be so afraid to show you've still got it."

"I don't know that I ever had it," she laughed. "This is so silly."

"Is not." I picked out a simple, black sheath and shooed her into the closet so she could try it on. I'd always envied the walk-in closet in the master bedroom—and it had only been half-filled since the divorce, giving her even more room.

Darcy and I exchanged a look that could only be described as exasperated while Mom changed into the dress. I looked over the pile of discarded dresses and wondered if we could donate them—or better yet, burn them.

"So this guy's pretty special, huh?" I called out as I picked through outfits I remembered from childhood.

"I'm pretty sure she wore that to your confirmation," Darcy whispered, pointing to a dress I was examining.

"Bob?" Mom called out, unaware of our giggles. "He's very sweet. A gentleman. You don't meet many of them nowadays."

"That's true, I guess. You've already met a few idiots." In the month since she'd decided to venture into the dating world again, Mom had proven to be fairly popular. And why not? She was still beautiful, a brilliant entrepreneur, and she made chocolate chip cookies to die for.

"Don't remind me. I don't want to think about any of them when I'm getting ready to see Bob."

Darcy ignored this, of course. "Gotten any calls from the

insurance guy?" He'd tried to sell Mom a life insurance policy between the appetizer and entrée courses.

"Only two. I think he finally got the message." And then there'd been the guy whose wife picked him up after dinner —they were in the process of splitting up but still living together and, evidently, still sharing a car.

I was glad this Bob person seemed like a decent guy, though I worried that her less-than-stellar experiences had made her lower her expectations to the point where anyone who didn't pose a threat or tell her she reminded him of his ex-wife or mother seemed like a catch.

The closet door opened and my jaw just about hit the floor. "Whoa. Mom. Holy cow." I held my head in my hands in case it decided to fall off.

"Mom! You're hot!" Darcy bounced on the bed hard enough to almost knock me on the floor.

Mom touched a trembling hand to her upswept blond hair, her cheeks going pink. "No, I'm not." She giggled, looking at the floor.

"But you are." I got up before Darcy knocked me on my butt and went to her. "You're always hiding your figure! Why? You look gorgeous." She had a perfect hourglass shape which my dress accentuated.

"I've seen Emma wear that dress and she's never looked that good in it."

I gave my sister a dirty look. "Thanks. Though you're right. But you didn't need to say it."

"Do I really look nice?" Mom asked, looking back and forth between us.

"You wanna know something?" I whispered. "I think you

know you do. I can tell. And I think Bob's gonna lose his mind when he sees you."

"Here." Darcy handed her a pair of red pumps. "Unless you think they're too daring for a third date."

"Shush." But she took the pumps because she wasn't stupid.

"I don't know if we can let you out of the house looking like this," I teased.

"What about poor Bob?" Darcy lobbed back with a wink. "I hope he doesn't have a bad heart. Maybe we should call him up and ask, just to be safe."

"I wanna see a doctor's report."

"Enough, you two," Mom laughed. "Go. I think I can handle putting on makeup and perfume."

"Go light on both," I advised. "You're already gonna knock him out. You want him to be able to come to eventually."

"Go, go." She shooed us out of the room, laughing softly. I couldn't get over how much younger she seemed. How much happier.

Which was why my sister surprised me by whispering, "It's a shame," as we passed our childhood bedrooms and walked downstairs.

"What is?" I whispered back.

"That she took this long to do this."

I could agree with that. "Hey, things happen when they're supposed to happen. Who knows why she was supposed to wait as long as she did? There had to be a reason. We'll find out eventually."

"Maybe this Bob guy is the one for her?" she suggested.

We puttered around the kitchen, which was where we both normally ended up. It was the heart of the house, especially since so many of Mom's recipes had been born there. Oh, the calories we'd consumed.

"I don't hate the idea, but let's not courage anything."

"Why not?" she asked, sitting on a stool at the counter. "You're the one who gave her the big idea to start dating. What's wrong with her finding the right guy?"

"I don't want her jumping into anything too soon, you know?" I sat across from her and pulled a chocolate chip cookie from the jar between us before breaking it in half.

Darcy eyed the cookie. "Well?"

"Well what?"

She held out her hand. "Are you gonna share?"

I blinked. "Um, no?"

"Normally, when a person breaks something in half, it's because they plan on sharing half with somebody else."

"That's nice." I licked both halves. "Get your own. Anyway, that's what bothers me. I don't want her jumping into anything with this Bob person just because he's the first nice guy who's come along. She's been trying to date for a month. Just one month."

"Yeah, but she's also a grown woman, not some little kid who needs to figure out the whole concept of dating and having a relationship. She knows about all that stuff." She took a cookie for herself and picked at it, thoughtful.

"That's true. I guess she knows better than anybody what she wants. Who she wants to be with."

"Besides," she added, "it's not like they're gonna get

married right away. I don't think she'd ever jump into that. Not after the divorce."

"Also true." I sighed, looking up at the ceiling like I could see through it and straight up into Mom's room. She was like a girl getting ready for a big dance—the sound of her happy humming floated our way through the thin floor. The walls and floors of the old house weren't exactly the thickest, which meant there was never any such thing as privacy when we were kids.

"What are you really upset about?" Darcy lowered her brow, looking at me in her usual no-nonsense, big sister way.

"I'm not upset."

"You are."

"Am not."

"Apprehensive, then. You're apprehensive. Why? You're usually one of the most positive people I know. You can take just about anything and turn it into a positive." She snickered. "Or bulldoze your way through it."

"I'm not a bulldozer."

"No. You drive one."

"You sound like Joe."

"Maybe Joe has a point."

"Shut up." I got up to wash my hands. "I don't even know why I ate that cookie. I'm supposed to be meeting him for ice cream later."

I pretended not to hear her snicker, but clearly I heard it because she wanted me to. "Ooh. Ice cream with the detective."

"Shut up," I said again. "It's not a date."

"I never said it was. You're the one who used that word."

"Whatever. You know what I'm trying to say. I'd appreciate you not trying to make this into something it isn't. I haven't spoken to him since I left for my trip to Austin, and he wanted to catch up."

"Mm-hmm."

I turned around and almost snapped a hand towel at her. "Enough. We're not here to talk about me. We're talking about Mom, remember?"

"Sure, sure. Whatever you say."

"Listen up." I shook the towel in her face. "I mean this. Don't act like there's anything between Joe and me. I don't need that in my life. Neither does he."

She stopped joking around, her blue eyes narrowing. "What's that mean?"

"He's been through a lot. I mean, a whole lot." I hadn't told her. I had never told anybody about Joe's past. But in the month since he'd moved from Paradise City to get his health in order and step away from the stress of his job, everybody in my life seemed more determined than ever to shove us together.

I dropped my voice to the barest whisper. "Promise you'll keep this to yourself." I then gave her a brief rundown. His wife, the accident. How he'd basically thrown himself into work since then.

Her face fell. "Oh, gosh. Poor guy. Why didn't you tell me before?"

"Because he obviously doesn't want lots of people to know. Maybe he's worried they'll feel sorry for him. I bet that's it, knowing the sort of person he is." I folded and refolded the towel just to have something to do. "I don't want people making a big deal about us being friends. He needs time. Heck, so do I. I don't want to start thinking of him that way and get all wrapped up with him when he might not be ready for anything like that. It's just as much for him as it is for me that I act stubborn and difficult about this. Okay?"

"Okay. Sure. I'll back off." There was a gleam in her eyes, though. "You do like him. Admit it."

"Of course I do. I'm not an idiot." Why bother pretending? It was easier to admit it to people I trusted, like my sister and my best friend Raina, than it was to act otherwise.

Mom's heels clicked on the wood floor as she approached. When she stepped into the kitchen, I pretended to swoon.

"Who's this supermodel?" Darcy asked.

"Stop." But our mother was glowing, absolutely radiant as she ran her hands down the length of the dress. "This really looks nice?"

"Beautiful," I confirmed, giving her two thumbs up. "And if things go well tonight and it's clear you two wanna see each other again, you have to invite Bob to visit the café so I can get a look at him."

"Yes, definitely," Darcy agreed. "I'm surprised he hasn't been in yet."

"His work keeps him busy," Mom explained. "Besides, I've wanted to avoid the gossip that you know will stir up if he comes in and people find out who he is."

I draped myself over the counter with a groan. "Wow. It's like she finally gets it."

CHAPTER TWO

"You know she won't stop spreading gossip just because she's dating somebody now." Joe snickered before taking a lick of his vanilla cone. Who chose vanilla when there were so many interesting flavors waiting to be tested?

"I can hope," I muttered, nibbling at my chocolate peanut butter swirl. There was a nice ribbon of peanut butter in there, which to me was the mark of a truly superior product.

Vanilla. Sheesh.

"It's nice that she's getting out, testing the waters."

We strolled down the boardwalk with Lola in the lead, hoping as always to get a bite of a discarded pizza crust or a few stray fries. Granted, she'd have a pretty tough time fighting against the seagulls who fought and squawked at each other, hovering over our heads only to dive bomb at the slightest hint of a feast.

But she'd just gotten her little cast taken off and wanted

to make up for lost time. I knew I would've been the same way in her place, so I had no room to judge her.

"Yeah, I know," I murmured, telling myself it was for the best that Mom was getting out in the world again.

"Hmm. You don't sound convinced. What's the matter?"

"Nothing," I insisted.

"You're not happy."

"I'm trying to manage this dog—who by the way is much stronger than her tiny size would lead you to believe, don't be fooled—and an ice cream cone at the same time. Would you be happy?"

"Here. Let me." He took the leash from me without asking. "Now. It's just you and the ice cream. What's the matter? Don't tell me you're against her dating."

"Not at all. I've wanted this for her for a long time, honestly. When she was getting ready tonight, she glowed. She was so happy. That whole part of her life has been closed off for so long. It's like watching somebody come out of a long sleep. She's shaking it off, she's waking up."

"So why do you still sound so low? I'm not Darcy. You can be upfront with me." He licked his ice cream, handling Lola with ease. To look at him, no one would believe he'd suffered a panic attack severe enough to land him in the hospital only five or six weeks prior. He was the picture of relaxation in his polo and jeans, his canvas sneakers slapping the boards.

"I'll tell you the same thing I told Darcy, actually. I don't love the idea of Mom jumping into something too fast. Just because this guy isn't smarmy or sketchy doesn't mean she needs to put all her eggs in his basket. So to speak."

"Who says she is?"

I shrugged. "I don't know. She really seems to like him. It's three dates now, and she's gonna encourage him to come to the café. I'd imagine that means she wants me and Darcy to get a look at him, and of course I want to. But doesn't that mean there's something more brewing?"

"It doesn't have to."

I stared off to my left, where falling darkness made the crashing waves more difficult to see. I could still hear them, though, even over the general hubbub around us. A swim would've been perfect right about now, fighting against the waves, letting them crash over me.

Why did I feel so twisted up inside over something that should've made me happy?

"I don't want her getting hurt again," I decided, and something about that felt right. Like I'd finally figured out what was bothering me and could put words to it.

"I know you don't, because you're a good person."

"Nobody would want their mother hurt," I argued.

"You know what I mean. You're an optimist, generally, but the people you care about are a different story. You love hard. You're all-in. That's admirable."

I couldn't help warming a little at the compliment. Yes, I was smitten—regrettably so. "You know what else bothers me?" I asked, since I didn't want this to become a compliment fest.

"The fact that I ordered vanilla ice cream?" When I shot him a surprised look, he grinned. "You looked at me like I lost my mind."

"I thought you did."

"Some people like vanilla ice cream, especially when it's really good quality. Look at those specks of vanilla. That's good stuff right there. It's fresh and clean and good."

"Hmph. Gimme a thick peanut butter ribbon any day. Anyway, what was I saying?"

"You were about to tell me what else bothers you." He pulled Lola away from a kid with what looked like a fried candy bar in time to prevent her from getting a mouthful of dripped chocolate. "No, Lola. No chocolate."

She looked back at him with what I could only think of as disgust. "For an animal who can't really do facial expressions, she's very good at putting a man in his place," he said with a smile.

"Good girl." I giggled. "Anyway, right. I worry she feels like she has to find a boyfriend now that Nell's dating somebody. And Dad's got the baby coming, of course. Trixie's always floating around the dating pool, seeing if anybody catches her eye. I worry she feels like she has to keep up, so she's going all-in on the first reasonable option that's come her way."

He didn't say anything for a long time, settling for finishing his cone and keeping Lola under control. I wondered if I'd hit a nerve. It was always so touchy, talking to him about things like this. Wondering when I was going to say the wrong thing.

I sort of had a talent for that as it was.

"You know what I think?" he finally asked.

I looked at him. The various flashing neon signs of the stores and restaurants on the boardwalk cast his strong profile in a pretty glow that contrasted with his serious expression. I started wishing I hadn't gotten us on this topic.

"What?" I prompted with my heart in my throat.

"I think if she's willing to try again, that means she's willing to accept the consequences—good and bad. It's been a few years since the divorce and she's finally ready to get out there. I wouldn't rain on her parade."

"Oh, gosh! No! I wouldn't do that. She has no idea what I'm thinking about this, honestly."

"Okay, good." The tension in his jaw melted away. "Otherwise, I think she can handle it. You've gotta let her enjoy herself. And if this guy turns out to be a jerk, you'll be there for her. If he's a good guy and he's good to her and she's happy being with him, what's the problem?"

"You're right, of course. I'm a worrywart."

"You're not. You're somebody who's been burned before, and you don't want her to get burned the way you did. There's nothing wrong with that. But maybe lighten up a little, huh?"

"Fine, fine. How are you? How's Cape Hope treating you?" I lowered my voice. "More importantly, how's my dad treating you?"

"He's great," Joe assured me with a grin. "Really. He showed me the ropes and lets me do my thing now. The most pressing case I've handled so far was who broke Mrs. Duffy's picket fence and got into her prize-winning roses."

"Those roses are more precious to her than her children."

"Yeah, no kidding." He laughed, rueful. "When she first called to report the crime—which was how she described it

—she was nearly hysterical. She threatened to sue Mr. Burke for letting his Doberman escape the yard and tear into hers."

"Well, gee." I rolled my eyes. "If the dog was able to break down her fence, he probably broke down his own fence, too."

"Bingo," he chuckled. "But lord, you would've thought we were on the case of who robbed Fort Knox."

"Still, it's a welcome change from Paradise City, isn't it?"

"No contest," he agreed. "God, I feel like I can breathe again. It's the same air down here as it is thirty minutes up the parkway, but it might as well be a different world."

"I'm glad for you. Really, I am."

"I owe it all to you."

"How so?"

He pulled Lola back from a group of giggling, bikini-clad girls who, I noticed, giggled harder when they got a look at the man walking with me.

"What a cute dog!" one of them exclaimed, bending down to pet Lola in an attempt to keep him around.

Who could blame them? He was even hot while wearing a polo, and not many men could pull that off.

"Isn't she?" I asked, taking the leash from him and guiding Lola away from the group.

"What was that about?" he said with a laugh, jogging to catch up to me.

"They were all too young for you," I hissed, glancing over my shoulder. More than one of them was in the process of giving me an absolutely filthy look, which I shot right back.

"What?" He laughed harder than before. "Uh, thanks, but I'm not in the market for an eighteen-year-old."

"Which would make you one of the few men on the boardwalk to feel that way."

"Whatever. Anyway, I owe it to you because I never would've come down here for a visit if you didn't recommend I take time away to get my stress under control. And when I visited, I decided this was the kind of place I could see myself spending more time in." He snickered. "Plus, if it wasn't for you getting yourself mixed up in that murder investigation, I never would've met you. Or your father, who happens to be the guy who pulled strings to get me transferred."

"I'm sure he's loving having you there."

"Oh, yeah. He can finally take a day off now and then. I don't know why he takes everybody's problems on himself, like the world will end if he's not on the job." He scratched his head with a quizzical expression. "Hmm. Who's that sound like?"

I didn't elbow him nearly as hard as I could have, since I was very mature. "What can I say? I'm a mix of both parents. I got Mom's sweet tooth and curiosity, and Dad's inability to walk away from a problem without trying to solve it. Which is why it kills me every time he tells me to stay out of trouble. What a hypocrite."

"You say hypocrite, I say concerned father."

"Either way, it's infuriating."

"At least there hasn't been much trouble lately. Chuck Welburn's all settled in now up at his new place. I ran into him when you were out of town and he asked about you. I think you have a fan. I know I'd be a fan if you discovered I was heir to a fortune I never knew about."

"What can I say?" I blew on my nails and buffed them on my shirt. "And Dad's a fan of my being the reason you ended up in town, so Holly will get off his back about being at work all the time. I wouldn't be surprised if she tries to talk him into retiring now that you're here to pick up the slack."

There I went again, running my mouth.

His face fell, then hardened into an unreadable mask.

I glanced his way once, twice, wishing I knew when to stop. "Not that anybody expects you to stay here forever. Nobody's trying to tie you down. I know this was only supposed to be temporary. I'm looking for the foot that fell out of my mouth." I raised my voice, looking around. "Has anybody seen the foot that fell out of my mouth just now?"

"Okay, okay." He stopped short of clamping a hand over my mouth, but just barely. "Enough. I don't know yet how I'm feeling about the long-term. It's still up in the air. For now, I'm enjoying being here and I feel like my life is becoming mine again. Can that be enough?"

"More than enough." My head bobbed up and down. I really needed to learn when to leave well enough alone, before I talked myself into a corner I couldn't get out of.

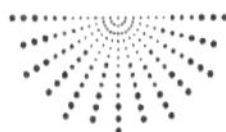

CHAPTER THREE

How did I know when Bob walked into the café without having ever seen him before that morning?

Easy. He was the guy whose face lit up when he laid eyes on my mother—who let out a choked little squeal when she saw him.

It knocked the breath out of my lungs, that single second of him seeing her and her seeing him. It was puppy love, like they were a pair of teenagers wondering when they could sneak away to make out a little when the grownups were busy doing grownup things.

Sure, that particular analogy made me gag just a little. I might've been an adult and well aware of adult things but this was still my mother I was thinking about.

It also made me happy, since he was clearly as into her as she was into him.

"That's Bob," she whispered, standing next to me behind the counter.

"No, duh," I whispered back, nudging her. "I think the

lights are burning a little brighter than they were before he walked in. Or it's just the way you're glowing."

"Shush," she warned before turning her attention to him.

I turned my attention in that direction, too, sizing him up. He was a good-looking man. Obviously, my mom was a babe, so that wasn't surprising. Tall, with black hair that was only just starting to thin a little and a physique that told me he tried to stay in shape. A golfer, maybe, or a runner.

He flashed a bright smile when he reached the counter. "Hi."

"Hi," Mom breathed. I wondered if she'd need an oxygen mask when this was all over.

"How are you?" he asked. Oh, jeez, he was so nervous. The cuteness was going to kill me. I wondered if either of them would notice if I collapsed right then and there.

"I'm fine." She beamed. "Happy to see you."

"Same here." He looked around with an appreciative smile. "So, this is your business." I was glad just about every table was filled, so he could see how popular Mom's café really was. He had come at the perfect time. We were past the rush, so Mom would have a little time to chat with him, but we weren't empty, either.

"This is it," she breathed. I could tell how proud she was. Heck, I was proud, too. I wanted him to see how successful she was, how substantial she was. How she wasn't somebody to be taken lightly, even with all her little quirks.

"I can see why people flock here. It's such a welcoming place. And so pretty." He winked at her in a roguish way. "Like the owner."

Dear Lord, I was either going to gag or combust. He was so smitten! No wonder Mom was nuts about him.

I cleared my throat. I'd been standing there the entire time, but neither of them acknowledged me. "Maybe I should scoot," I suggested, looking from one of them to the other.

Mom slapped a hand to her forehead. "My goodness, I'm sorry. Emma, this is Bob Perlman. Bob, this is my daughter, Emma." She said it with no shortage of motherly pride, which was nice. Nobody wanted to see their mother wince as she introduced them.

"I'm so sorry! How rude of me. Of course, you look exactly alike!" He held his hand over the counter for me to shake, and I appreciated the firmness of his grip, the way he maintained eye contact. "It's a pleasure to meet you."

"Likewise. My sister and I have been dying to get a look —I mean, to meet you. Mom has said such nice things." I felt her hot, burning glare on the side of my head.

But he didn't seem to notice my little faux pas. Probably too busy being enamored with my mother to care very much. "I, uh, ought to check the oven. Excuse me."

There was nothing in the oven, but something told me my mother would shove me in if I didn't give them a little time alone.

I dashed back to the kitchen. Lola raised her head from her bed, more annoyed at being woken from her second nap of the day than anything else, I guessed. "Pardon me, your highness," I whispered as I darted across the room. "Keep up the good work of making sure your bed doesn't fly away." I then ducked out the café's back door before ducking through the back door of Darcy's shop, just next door.

"Quick!" I waved frantically from the back of the store, to where my sister stood behind the counter. "He's over there now!"

She practically flew over the counter with barely so much as a glance toward the kid she had working with her that day. "I'll be right back!" she pledged.

"What do you think?" she whispered as we ducked back into the café through the kitchen and disturbed the dog for a second time.

"I think they're both so taken with each other, the café could fall down around their heads neither of them would notice." We peeked in through the open kitchen door in time to see Bob take Mom's hand while staring sweetly. She giggled like a young girl, raising her other hand to her cheek as it flushed.

"I wonder what he said?" Darcy whispered.

"Whatever it was, she's practically ready to take flight."

"Does he seem like a nice guy?"

"He seems nice enough. We barely exchanged more than a couple of words. But he likes her a lot, and she's clearly crazy about him. Maybe that has to be enough for now."

At some point, Mom must have left her blissful state long enough to notice her daughters whispering. "Get out here, both of you," she said with a laugh. "Honestly, peeking out from inside the kitchen, having a little whisper session. You're entirely too much!" In another second, she would pull out a fan and snap it open to cool herself before she caught the vapors. It wouldn't have surprised me if she'd put on a southern accent to really drive home the genteel effect.

He exchanged pleasantries with Darcy and the four of us chatted about the café, the bookstore, and my work before he checked his watch. "I'm sorry, I need to get going. I have a quick meeting here in town, but I'd love to see you again. Tonight." He cast a hopeful look Mom's way.

"Come on," Darcy murmured, taking me by the hand and practically dragging me away. "It was nice to meet you, Bob. We hope to see you again soon." I barely had time to nod in agreement before my sister yanked me into the kitchen and swung the door shut behind us.

"So? What did you think?" I asked, while peering out the round, glass window cut into the door. They were like a couple of kids, laughing softly together as Mom walked him outside.

"He seems nice. And like you said, he's obviously smitten. I hope we can all get together and spend a little more time getting to know him, though," Darcy pointed out.

"I'm sure that will come in time." I glanced away from the window with a smirk. "We never wanted to bring our boyfriends home for dinner this soon, did we?"

She snorted at the memory. "Yeah, but we knew we'd be having dinner with a detective who happened to be our father, who happened to never shrink away from asking embarrassing questions."

"Hey, I could always invite Joe if we want to let Mom feel sort of pressure we used to," I suggested, laughing.

"Sure, and that wouldn't backfire in your face at all, would it?" She left to return to her shop, and I left the kitchen in time to find my mother practically floating in from the sidewalk.

"Well?" she asked as she rejoined me. There were practically hearts in place of where her eyes used to be. The woman had turned into an emoji.

"He's very handsome," I grinned. "And obviously very taken with you."

She waved a hand like I was putting her on, but she didn't stop smiling like a goon. "We like each other. What's so bad about that?"

"I never said there was anything bad about it. In fact, I think it's great." I kissed her cheek and noted the scent of a man's cologne on her skin and clothes. So I wasn't the only one to give her a kiss. It was touching and funny and awkward all at once.

We talked more about this as the day went on, while customers came and went. He was semiretired, having once owned a chain of successful hardware stores which he then sold to a larger company for a pretty penny. Since then, according to my mother, he'd been dabbling in real estate and private equity investments. I couldn't help but admit he sounded like a fairly substantial guy.

And practically the opposite of my blue-collar father.

"He loves the theater and art and music. He's well-traveled, he's well-read. I'm sure he and Darcy would have so much to talk about when it comes to books."

"Hey, I'm not illiterate," I teased, restocking the bakery case.

The woman was too far-gone to care, probably imagining an intimate wedding at the house. "Of course, of course. And when I told him what you do for a living, he was very impressed and curious to learn more."

"Hey, maybe he can give me some ideas for new assignments to pitch my editor, since he's so well-traveled." I didn't really think so, but I could tell it made Mom happy to hear me speaking positively about her beau.

It was early afternoon and I was about to beg off for the rest of the day—it never got very busy after a certain point, and I had work to do—when the bell above the door chimed. Trixie Graham floated into the café in all her glory. Her leopard print caftan was completely on-brand, floating around her in dramatic fashion as she approached the counter. I'd seen the excitement in her eyes enough times to know she had a big, juicy piece of gossip to share.

And she shared it without delay. "Did you hear there was a body found floating in the bay this morning?" she asked, scandal throbbing in her voice. She could already see the headline, I knew, and naturally the story would be written by her.

Mom chuckled, shaking her head at her best friend. "You come in here with the most morbid stories, and you deliver them like the happiest news anyone ever heard."

"Well, I'm not saying I'm glad a woman died, but this means plenty of work for me. Ever since the excitement over Charlie Welborn died down, I've been looking for something new to report on." Naturally, Trixie had written all about Charlie finding the truth of his parentage after seventy years.

She turned to me with a wink. "This sounds like the sort of case your fella could sink his teeth into."

I barely bit back a sigh of frustration. She meant well, but I didn't need her blabbing to everybody about us. "Not my fella," I reminded her in a singsong voice. "Besides, he's not the only detective in town."

"Just the same. I'm sure he'll be glad to have something to do for once, since this town is normally so boring."

"Newsflash. He came here because it was so boring. He needed a break before he suffered a nervous collapse or whatever." I dished her up a slice of carrot cake, her favorite, and handed it over with a syrupy sweet smile. "But I'm sure he would be flattered to know you have so much faith in his abilities."

"Those are hardly the abilities I care most about." She winked.

I had to admire her zest for life, which was the only thing that kept me from telling her to invest in a hormone suppressant. "Regardless, I hope they find out what happened soon, since you know half the town will be dying to know. And the other half will be worried to death that there's a serial killer on the loose."

She dipped her fork in the to-die-for cream cheese frosting and licked it off. "Sounds like a case for my favorite amateur sleuth."

"No, thank you," I was quick to reply, shaking my head. "No, my sleuthing days are over. I've had one close call too many, thank you very much, and I have more than enough work to keep me busy."

Famous last words.

CHAPTER FOUR

The thing about the best-laid plans was how often they went awry. Whoever said that had it right.

I had to wonder when the phone rang hours later, while I was hard at work at my dining room table, whether the person who coined that saying had ever met my mother. Impossible, of course, since that saying was much older than she was.

Still, it was uncanny how she managed always to catch me right when I was deeply involved in my work.

"Darn it," I whispered when the phone rang, making a point to save my document before fishing around for the phone. I was already up against a deadline for my Austin pieces and didn't have a lot of time to discuss what Mom should wear for her next date.

"Mom, I'm super busy," I informed her on answering. "I don't want to be rude, but—"

"I can't get a hold of him." It was like I had never said a word. Sometimes I had to wonder if I only imagined speaking, since she was so good at pretending never to hear a word.

"What?" I asked, holding the bridge of my nose between my thumb and forefinger. I knew that tone in her voice. She was fretful, deeply upset.

"Bob. I can't get a hold of Bob. He said he wanted to get together tonight, but I have no idea what he has in mind for what time or anything. He's not answering his phone or responding to messages."

Just then, I wanted to kill Bob. If he was jerking her around… "Maybe something came up," I suggested for her sake. "I wouldn't get too excited just yet. He said he had a meeting, right?"

"It was supposed to be a quick meeting, and it was hours ago. He's been MIA since then. I just know something happened."

"You don't know any such thing. Don't jump to conclusions—you don't need to stress yourself out like this." At the same time, I wondered how long it would take to learn his address and drive to his house and demand an explanation. No way was he going to jerk my mom around after it had taken her so long to work up to this point.

"I have a bad feeling, is all," she murmured. "Maybe it would've been better to never start this dating thing."

I didn't know what to do. My instinct was to comfort her, to tell her the sort of things a person told someone they cared about when something like this happened. To remind her how nice he seemed, how he'd smiled from ear to ear when he saw her, how sweet they were together.

On the other hand, would that only hurt her in the end if

he ghosted her? I didn't want to inadvertently rub salt in the wound. There was little for me to say without knowing for sure what his intentions were.

"I'm sure it's fine," I settled on repeating. "He might've forgotten. Or maybe something came up and he just never got the chance to let you know. Or he might have gone home and decided to take a nap and left his ringer on silent. Who knows?"

"Yes, I guess so." She didn't sound convinced.

Then again, neither was I. "Give him another call and let him know you're disappointed. Definitely tell him you're annoyed with him. He needs to know this is unacceptable going forward."

"You're right." I was glad to hear firmness in her voice. "I'm not going to let him jerk me around, no matter how nice he is." Pretty soon, she'd break out into a chorus of *I Am Woman*, but I would rather have heard that than a rousing rendition of *Emma, Why Did You Let Me Do This*.

"There you go. Set him straight right away. You have standards. You're not the sort of person who will wait around, hoping he decides you're worthy of a phone call. You're Sylvia Harmon, successful entrepreneur and a total babe."

"I don't know about that last part." She chuckled. It was clear from her tone of voice that she was already in a better mood.

"Please. I remember how you looked last night. Did his tongue fall out of his mouth when he first saw you or what?" I teased.

"Emma," she warned, but there was a giggle in her voice that gave her away.

"Mm-hmm," I teased. "I thought so."

"You are incorrigible."

"Says the woman who raised me," I reminded her. "Give him a call. Even if he doesn't answer, you'll feel better if you set him straight via voicemail."

"You're right. I'll do that." She sounded much better when she got off the phone than she had when she first called, which made me feel better.

But not for long.

Just who did this guy think he was? Being all nice and polite, making my mother care about him. And what did he turn around and do? He fell off the face of the earth.

I didn't want to be right. I didn't want my fears and apprehensions to be right. I wanted her to be happy.

The roll I'd been on with my work had ground to a total stop, and I groaned as I stood to stretch. There were times when I considered putting my phone on the Do Not Disturb setting so nobody could bother me while I was working. It wasn't easy getting into a groove, and even more difficult to get back into it once it had been brought to a stop.

Then again, I would've missed Mom's call if I had done that. She would currently be spiraling out of control, convinced the first nice guy she'd met since her divorce had been toying with her all along. Yes, she would've had herself worked up into a real frenzy.

And how would that have been your problem? Strange, how Joe Sullivan had managed to work his way into my subconscious. He popped up every now and then, asking questions I knew he would've asked me in real life if given the opportunity. *Why is everybody else's problem your problem?*

Gosh. He even sounded smug in my head.

I didn't know the answer to that question. If he'd asked, I would've countered with something about caring too much. Was that such a crime? And we would've argued, and I would have felt terrible in the end.

Because part of me would've known he was right. I would never say that to him, of course. He'd never let me live it down.

Everyone else's problem didn't need to be mine. This was something I was trying to work on. Really, I was. Ever since Lola's accident and what might've happened if we hadn't all been so lucky, I'd been thinking about a lot of things. The chances I took, the amount of time I spent working to solve other people's problems when I should've been working on my own.

Such as the articles that were currently waiting for me to finish them before sending them to my editor so I could get paid. "I have to keep you happy, don't I?" I asked Lola, scratching her behind the ears. She was at that moment on her fourth nap of the day, and as always shot me a doleful look for interrupting her slumber. "Excuse me, Princess." I snickered before turning back to my open document.

But no matter how determined I was to focus on writing about Austin's food scene, there was no shaking the suspicion that something truly was wrong. What was it about this Bob person? He seemed so nice, had even appeared genuinely glad to meet us.

Though part of me wondered if he wasn't a little spooked, having met us so early in the game. Maybe he was backing off because he felt pressured. If was the case, I would feel bad, but I'd also want to slap him around.

For one thing, Darcy and I were awesome. We were also adults, adults who required nothing of him aside from being nice to their mother. He couldn't even manage to do that.

No, no. I had to keep myself from going down that road. This could all be explained away so simply. Hadn't I already given Mom examples of what could have been the problem?

It was one thing to say those things in the hope of easing her mind. It was another thing to actually believe them, which I really didn't. He'd seemed sincere in wanting to see her again that night.

Either something bad had happened, or he was a very good actor.

My fingers twitched, but not the way I needed them to. I needed to get back to work, to type until the words blurred in front of my eyes. Instead, I kept glancing at my phone, wanting to call Joe of all people. I wanted to inform him that I'd been right all along, that Mom had jumped into catching feelings for this guy way too soon.

I would then ask if he knew anywhere for me to hide a body so nobody could ever find it.

I was so deep in this little fantasy of murdering Bob that the buzzing of my phone made me jump in surprise.

"Now, what are the odds of that?" I murmured to Lola, who couldn't have cared less, when I saw it was Joe who was calling.

"I was right. This Bob guy's a real jerk," I grumbled.

A pause. "Um, hello to you, too. I'm doing fine. How are you?"

"Yeah, yeah. I'm rude. We both knew this. Anyway, Mom is freaking out because Bob dropped off the face of the earth since this morning, when they were supposed to get together tonight. Now she's got me concerned and wondering where to hide his body."

"Yeah, I figured that out. Actually, that's why I'm calling you."

"Wait. Why would you be calling me because of her?"

"Not because of her. At least, not technically. No, it is technically because of her. God, I can't even think straight right now."

"What you talking about?" I stood, and immediately started to pace the room. "What's wrong with Mom?"

"It's not what's wrong with her, per se." I realized the strained tone in his voice had returned, the tone I'd become familiar with during our dealings in Paradise city. He sounded like his old self, like all of the relaxation he'd earned in Cape Hope had melted away.

And it made me sad for him.

But it didn't give me patience. "Just come out with it. What's going on?"

"Did you hear about the body that was found in the bay?"

"Of course. Trixie told us about it today, but that's all I heard since I went home right after that."

"I figured if you'd been working in the café, you would know about it by now. I just questioned someone in connection with this woman's death. They were seen together early yesterday evening."

"Okay. Still wondering what this has to do with my mother."

"Why don't you try letting me finish?" And there was that snappy tone of his. I sure hadn't missed it. "I'm trying to break this as gently as I can, and you keep making it difficult."

"Okay. Go ahead." Meanwhile, my fist was clenched tight enough that my nails dug into my palm.

"The man I just questioned wasn't with the victim for very long, at least according to him." He then took a deep breath and let it out slowly enough that I was convinced he was torturing me. Just as I was about to scream, he continued. "After he left her, he went to dinner. With your mother."

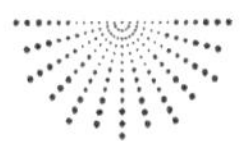

CHAPTER FIVE

"For the record, this is a terrible idea."

"For the record, no it isn't." I glared at Joe, standing beside me on Mom's front porch.

He scowled. "For the record, she's gonna see me and think Bob was in an accident."

"For the record, would you rather jump out and scream *Boo*? Because that wouldn't give her a heart attack or anything."

Mom flung the door open, and I immediately thrust a bottle of wine I'd brought along in her direction. "Hi!" I shouted like she just lost her hearing.

"Oh, no." She put her other hand to her head. "I knew it. He was in an accident, wasn't he?"

Joe cleared his throat in a very obvious, very smug way. I chose to ignore him rather than engage, turning to Mom instead. "No, he wasn't. But we do need to talk to you about him."

"What is it? Does he have three wives? A stable of mistresses? Did he steal the real Bob Perlman's identity?" She just about slumped against the doorframe as she recited this litany of potential woes.

"No, no." I guided her into the house as gently as I could with Joe following. "No, it's nothing like that. But there is a problem."

"How about I open the bottle?" Joe asked. If I hadn't been getting myself ready to deeply disappoint my mother, I would've laughed at how uncomfortable he was.

Mom didn't hand the bottle over, however. "Just tell me. Get it out. Why did you come? What's wrong with Bob?"

I took the bottle from her and handed it to Joe, jerking my head toward the kitchen. For one thing, it would be better if she wasn't holding the wine; she'd probably drop it on the floor, and wasted wine was a terrible thing.

Also, I didn't feel like having to clean it up.

For another thing, it would be better if I told her this alone at first. I took Mom's hands and sat down with her. "Keep in mind as I tell you this that he's not actually in any trouble."

"What did he do?" she breathed, her eyes almost as big as the lenses to the reading glasses she was wearing.

I practically bent over backward, trying to come up with a good way to put it. "The police aren't sure yet if he did anything. But the woman who was found dead today was last seen with Bob last night, before you two went to dinner."

I kept a tight grip on her hands, both to support her and to, I hoped, keep her from picking up anything and throwing it. What would she think when she found out the man she liked so much was a suspect in a murder investigation?

Of all the times for me to be right about somebody, I wished it wasn't this time. I wanted so much for him to be a nice person, to be just what she needed. She'd waited so long.

"You can't be serious." Her voice was flat, completely without inflection. "You're making this up."

"Mom, I wish I was. That's where he was earlier, when you were worried about what might've happened. He didn't call because he was at the police station with Joe."

She shook her head. "No. No! How could he do such a thing? That jerk! That liar! I'll kill him!"

While I appreciated her passion, I couldn't help but wonder about her choice of words. She would kill him for possibly having killed somebody else? It seemed out of place. "Why would you do that? And why are you calling him a liar?"

She blinked rapidly, so fast I thought she might be about to faint. "Because he told me he wasn't seeing anybody else!"

It was my turn to almost swoon. "What are you talking about?"

"He was with another woman! What do you mean, what am I talking about? Good gosh!" She bolted up from the sofa and started pacing just like I'd been doing earlier. "On another date. Twice in the same night! And there I was, going to all that trouble to look nice for him! He didn't deserve it."

Joe entered the room carrying two wine glasses and the

uncorked bottle, but came to a dead stop at the sight and sound of my mother having a fit. Our eyes met. I shrugged, mouth hanging open. Mom was normally a little flighty, a little unpredictable. But this?

"Mom, no offense, but I think you're concerned about the wrong thing. I just got done telling you he was questioned in a murder investigation, and you're worried about him seeing somebody else? Doesn't the whole murder things seem a little more pressing?"

Words couldn't describe the withering look she shot me, but I might as well have been an ant on the floor. "Oh, come on. That's ridiculous. He's no more capable of murder than I am."

"That's funny, considering that you just threatened to kill him." I gladly took one of the two glasses from Joe and allowed him to fill it halfway. There I was, thinking she was the one who would need a drink. I should've known better.

"You know it's one thing to say something like that and another to do it. If that wasn't the case, you would've killed that philandering boyfriend of yours."

I gulped down half the glass in one shot.

Joe picked that moment to step in, and bless him for it. "Please, believe me. I don't like coming to your home with this sort of news. But the facts are the facts. Bob Perlman was seen with the victim yesterday evening. He's the last person she was seen with. This morning, her body was found floating in the bay where the two of them were seen on one of the docks nearby. I'm sorry, but those are the facts." He handed Mom the other glass, half-full.

"That doesn't prove anything," she informed him in a lofty tone. "I realize I don't do police work for a living, but even I know nothing you told me amounts to actual evidence. He was seen with her, but I met him for dinner at seven o'clock, and her body was found this morning. That's an awfully long time in between. Anything could've happened."

He rubbed the back of his neck, grinning ruefully. "I know. Trust me."

"I'm sorry, then, if I find it hard to believe based on the limited connection you provided that Bob would actually have murdered anyone. He's just not that type of person." She sat in an armchair, as prim as anything, crossing her legs at the knee and taking a dainty sip of her wine.

I finished mine, on the other hand, and considered going in for more. "I want to believe you. I really, really do. I don't want him to be a murderer. Especially not now that I've seen the two of you together. You're adorable. And yeah, from the limited contact I had with him today, he seems like a nice guy."

I sat nearby, facing her with my hands folded like I was praying. Maybe I was, on some level. I needed for her to understand. "But Mom, you have to get used to the idea of him not being who he said he was. If he was dating this other woman who died, that right there is a red flag. Really, truly bright red, big as life. What else did you not know, then? It's not like he would come out and tell you he had a habit of murdering people."

Again, she shot me a look. "Emma, I realize that you and your sister think I am a very silly person."

My head snapped back almost hard enough to give me whiplash. "No! And where is this even coming from?"

"I say that to remind you of your low opinion of my common sense. I know you and your sister think I don't possess any, but I do. I've also lived in this world a lot longer than you have, and I think I understand people. Goodness knows, I work with them every single day. I can tell you exactly who has a secret, who is unhappy. Sometimes, I can even tell why. For more than two decades, people have been my stock in trade. I know Bob is incapable of murder. I feel it."

She was so sincere, it almost made me want to cry. "I know you feel what you feel. But I would rather you adjust your expectations now, rather than being stunned to find he did maybe kill that woman—even if it was an accident. Do you know what I mean? I don't want you setting yourself up to get hurt."

She leaned in, eyes narrowed shrewdly. "Let me ask you. What made you so certain that Robbie Klein wasn't a murderer?"

She would go and bring that up. "Sure, but I knew Robbie longer than you've known Bob."

"An entire summer, ten years ago?" Mom shook her head, clicking her tongue. "That isn't a very strong history of knowing somebody. How did you know?"

"Instinct, then. Okay? Is that what you want to do here? I knew instinctively that he couldn't do anything like that. Congratulations."

"Thank you," she murmured. "My instincts are telling me the same thing about Bob. Even if we'd only met a few times socially, as friends, I would tell you the same thing I'm telling you now. This has nothing to do with us seeing each other. He doesn't have a violent bone in his body."

"Mrs. Harmon, I want that to be true. Really, I do." Joe shrugged. "However, murderers don't have to have a history of violence. Look at Deirdre Price. She had no sort of violent history, yet she pushed a man to his death. Then, she tried to shoot Emma and her agent rather than face the consequences. When someone is desperate, they're capable of anything. Sometimes, people make terrible mistakes they can't take back. That doesn't make them bad people, but it does mean they have to face what they did and pay the consequences."

Her smile was unflinching. "I'm sorry. I understand what you're saying, and I appreciate you coming here to tell me yourself. But I can't believe Bob would do something like that. And nothing you say will convince me otherwise."

Joe looked at me as if there was anything I could do about this.

"Okay, so stubbornness runs in the family," I admitted.

"It practically gallops, to borrow a line from an old movie," he replied with a scowl.

"I'm just saying, once we Harmon women believe in somebody, we don't like to be told otherwise."

"Be that as it may, it doesn't help me with my job." He turned to Mom, and I could see he was struggling to maintain his composure. I almost reminded him to be aware of his breathing, like he learned in the yoga class we'd attended together, but I didn't feel like taking my life in my hands. "Can you tell me what you and Bob did together last night? I need to corroborate the alibi he gave earlier."

"We had dinner reservations at seven o'clock. He was right on time." She even sounded proud of this, like it was a mark in his favor. All I wanted to do just then was wrap her up in a big hug and shield her from the world; she was way too good for it.

"And where was this dinner?"

"We went to Lou's."

"And how long were you there for, approximately?"

"I think it was around nine o'clock when we left. We lost track of time," she explained with a soft laugh. That laugh almost broke my heart. It was clear they'd had a nice time together. I hated to think of her tarnishing the memory of that date by imagining him seeing another woman before he'd seen her.

Or possibly killing that woman, but she didn't seem too concerned with that.

"Did you part ways there?" I noticed then that Joe kept looking at me, like he was gauging my reaction. Or waiting for one.

Mom cleared her throat, then looked down at the floor. I closed my eyes, my teeth clenched. I understood what all of Joe's looks were about. Bob had already given him the rundown. "Yes, I mean, no. We didn't. We came back here for a while."

I wanted to crawl out of my skin.

"And, um, around what time did he leave you?" I sneaked a peek at Joe from my half-closed eyes and found that he looked like he wanted to crawl out of his own skin, too.

Poor, flustered Mom. "Uh, I don't quite know. I didn't check the time."

"Oh, for gosh sakes, Mom. Just tell him. Jeez, Louise." I didn't mean for it to come out like I was angry, but enough was enough already. My mother was an adult, and I had sent her off in my best black dress, so what did I expect?

"Around two-thirty." She sounded like she was humiliated, while I was almost sort of impressed with old Bob. About a dozen questions ran through my head, but I decided against asking them. Even I had my limits.

"Thank you." Joe exhaled, his shoulders sagging. "That's not something I want to repeat ever again."

"You?" I snickered.

"All right, enough." Mom took a markedly longer sip of her wine this time. "Now, you know he wasn't lying when he told you where he was last night after being with that woman, whoever she was."

"Her name was Moira Banks. Is that name familiar to you?"

"Banks? Was she any relation to Nicholas Banks?"

Joe nodded. "His widow, yeah."

"I can't say I ever met her personally, but Lawrence was sort of a big deal for a while, wasn't he? Banking?" Mom shrugged. "Funny, with his name being Banks. Anyway, that's as much as I could tell you."

"While I'm glad your description of the evening matches Bob's," Joe continued, looking just as embarrassed as ever, "that doesn't mean he didn't do what it seems he might have done beforehand."

"I can imagine how he could have done anything like that before we—" Mom looked away, and so did I.

"For the record," Joe murmured, "I knew this was going to happen."

"Nobody likes a know-it-all," I hissed.

Mom's voice was plaintive. "Emma. Can you go talk to him? If I give you his address, I mean? I'm sure there has to be an explanation for all of this."

I turned back to my mother, astounded that she would even ask me to do something like that. "You've surprised me in the past, but this is the one to top everything. Why on earth would I go and talk to that man?"

"I would do it myself, but I'm embarrassed. I just found out he was probably seeing someone else underlying to me. I don't want to face him."

"Mom, this is so weird. I don't know if I can do this. Just the thought of it makes me so uncomfortable." Yet all I had to do was look at her and see how stricken she was, and how determined she was not to believe Bob capable of the things he was being accused of.

Why did I have to be such a softy?

"Okay. I'll go see him in the morning." I then looked at Joe, waiting for him to argue. When he didn't say anything for a while, I prompted, "Is there any problem with that?"

He sighed, looking up at the ceiling. "I'm supposed to say yes. I know I'm supposed to say yes."

"No, you want to say yes. There's no reason why I can't go to his house as the daughter of the woman he's dating and simply ask him what the heck the deal is. That's all I'll do," I added, holding up my right hand and making a cross of my chest with the left.

"I know I'm supposed to say yes," he repeated anyway.

I stuck my tongue out at him. "Sorry, Detective, you're just going to have to trust me."

He rubbed his temples, his eyes sliding shut. "Didn't I take this job so I could avoid stress?"

CHAPTER SIX

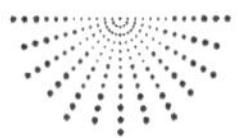

Bob Perlman lived on the Crest, fifteen minutes from Cape Hope. It was a super fancy, semi-secluded beach town. Most of the nicer homes in Cape Hope had long since been converted to businesses like bed and breakfasts, galleries, office space while these sprawling Victorians still served as private homes.

In other words, I was salivating by the time I reached the pale yellow, three-story home that looked like something out of a fairy tale. The happy, magical house where the heroine lived before everything went wrong and her wicked stepmother decided to turn her into a servant.

My mood was still pretty dark, even though the sight of so many gorgeous buildings in an absolutely breathtaking town set my imagination on fire and I wondered if my pink Bug made me stick out like a sore thumb among so many luxury cars. It probably did.

If this man wasn't who he made himself out to be, he had an earful coming his way no matter how beautiful and charming and idyllic his house was. No way was I going to let him get away with breaking my mother's heart. It had taken her so long to trust again.

I'd already called to ask if I could stop by. Not only did I not feel like making the drive, short as it was, if he wasn't home, but I didn't want him to feel like he was being bombarded. If Mom was right and he didn't do this terrible thing, he didn't deserve to feel threatened or harassed.

Even if I wanted to smack him for lying. If he'd actually lied. What a tangled web.

I found him sitting on the porch, half-hidden by tall hedges. Gone was the easy breezy confidence of the man I'd met just yesterday. He seemed to have shrunk several inches, but that could've been the effect of his slumped posture. He looked beaten, in other words.

I reminded myself this might have been an act. If he were a cold-blooded killer—or even somebody who had accidentally done something he couldn't take back—he'd make it a point to play on my sympathy. He would want to be the victim, the bewildered man who had no idea how any of this had happened.

I steeled myself for the possibility of this while climbing the wide, plank steps up to the porch. They were flanked on either side with potted flowers and cheerful pink, white, yellow.

Somehow, he already didn't fit the image of a murderer. And again, I forced myself to put this out of my mind. It didn't matter how nice his house was, how well-maintained. Deirdre Price had been the image of success and composure.

And she'd tried to kill me. And it wouldn't have been an accident if she'd gone through with it.

"Can I offer you something to drink? Coffee, tea?" he asked as I took a seat next to him, a wicker table between us. Bottled water sat in an ice-filled metal bucket on top, and a plate of cookies sat beside it. He'd thought of everything.

The cookies did nothing for me. I was obviously feeling some type of way if the sight of butter cookies weren't enough to catch my interest. "Just water, thank you." I'd already had my coffee for the morning. Besides, my nerves were jumpy enough as it was.

He nodded, sitting back with what looked and smelled like herbal tea. "Thank you for reaching out and coming to see me. I've been trying to come up with a way to explain myself to your mother, but I keep coming up short."

"I'm sure you can imagine how upset she was when she found out what happened." *Yes, Emma. Diplomacy. Maturity.* I'd let him do all the talking. He didn't need me to provide motive or excuses for him.

"I know how it must sound when I say this, but I feel like I have to." He placed his cup and saucer on the table and turned to me wearing a stern expression. "She's the person I'm most concerned about right now."

I bit back an impatient sigh. He knew how it must've sounded to say that? Then why had he bothered to say it? Anybody could say something like that. It didn't mean anything. "Don't you think you should be a little more concerned about yourself?" I asked, toying with the plastic bottle I held, for lack of anything better to do with my hands.

The look on his face brought my mother to mind. She was just as skilled at putting on the innocent act. Though I had to wonder if it was really an act. Maybe he was a little slow on the uptake.

"Why? I know I didn't kill Moira. When we parted ways, she was perfectly healthy and very much alive." He blinked his wide, innocent eyes. "I know I didn't kill her. I haven't been very concerned about myself at all since I heard what happened."

"Maybe you should get concerned," I suggested. "I don't mean to be rude. But this looks pretty serious. You were the last person seen with her. At least, that's how it looks right now. And the fact that you were seeing two women at the same time, I hate to tell you, but that doesn't look good, either. That's the sort of thing a jury takes into consideration whether they want to admit it or not."

He frowned, tilting his head to the side. "I wasn't seeing Moira. At least, not anymore. Not for quite a while. Is that the impression you got? That I was on a date with her? Not at all!"

"That's very much the impression I got," I murmured. It wasn't easy, trying to remain objective. Trying to stay strong when I really, truly wanted to believe him for Mom's sake.

"I know that's what the detective wants to believe. That Sullivan person." All things considered, I decided to forgive him for sounding so annoyed when he mentioned Joe. Lord knew, I understood what it meant to be completely frustrated by him, to feel like he wasn't doing as good a job as he could've done. I'd certainly felt that way when he was investigating Robbie Klein.

"If it wasn't a date, what was it?"

He snickered. "What? Can't a man meet with a woman without there being some sort of romantic relationship going on? The fact is, Moira and I were once an item, and not even a very serious one. Like I said, that ended a long time ago." Funny, but he sounded relieved to say it. If he'd wiped the back of his hand across his forehead and let out a sigh of relief, it would have fit his tone of voice perfectly.

"How long were you seeing each other?"

"Off and on for roughly a year. Believe me," he was quick to add when I winced, "it was very casual. We were never serious. She was often out of town for one reason or another. We might get together for dinner every once in a while. Before long, I had the feeling she wanted to take things to the next level, so to speak." He shook his head slowly. "I couldn't see doing that."

"Why not? From what I've heard of her, she was a pretty wealthy widow." From my preliminary internet researching, I'd found she was also very attractive. Polished. Well-groomed, perfectly accessorized. Granted, the pictures I'd seen usually involved her attending some sort of social function or whatever, but I doubted she became a slob in her personal life.

He looked at me like I'd just grown a second head. "And?" he asked. "Not only do I not need the money, but there's more to life than that. From what your mother told me about you, I didn't think you would find that sort of thing so important."

I didn't rise to the bait, if it was bait at all. "I didn't say I would've married her for her money. But some people would."

"I'm not some people," he informed me. "No, that didn't interest me at all, and she was unhappy when she figured that out. I guess the reason we never got serious was the fact that we had nothing in common except for running in the same social circle for a number of years. I knew her husband, at least vaguely. A part of my extended network. But we weren't friends, not really. When we spent time together, it was always... I don't know. Stilted. Formal, almost. I couldn't relax around her."

He looked out over his immaculate front lawn, sighing. "That's what I enjoy so much about your mom, you know. I'm sorry if you're uncomfortable with me bringing her up, but I feel like you need to know that. She's a wonderful woman. Warm and kind. The exact opposite of Moira, in fact. Everything was about appearance for her. She always seemed rather bored with me. And I was bored with her. That was the extent of our relationship."

"Then why did you meet with her two days ago? It doesn't sound like there was much warmth between you two."

"To be honest, it had to do with business. I realize that might be difficult to believe."

"Not so difficult," I allowed.

"I already told the detective about this. I invested some money with her husband, her late husband that is, before he passed. The investment is still paying dividends, or at least it was until recently. I wanted to discuss that with someone who might have answers, but for the life of me, I never could get a hold of the managers for the fund. She was one of the managers, if only in name, so in a sort of desperate move, I asked her to meet me. I didn't tell her why at the time."

"She probably wasn't too happy when she found out it was a business meeting," I mused. And I regretted it, because I was giving him an out. If they argued for some reason, he could blame it on that. I had to stop telling his story for him.

He shook his head, snickering. "No, she wasn't. In fact, she was outraged. Not only because I hadn't told her why I wanted to meet. She took it personally, like I was accusing her of stealing money. Believe me, that hadn't even occurred to me. I didn't think she had that much to do with the fund's management. Like I said, she was nominally involved. But I had to start somewhere. There hadn't been a report on the fund in two quarters. Again, that was unusual, since the reports came in like clockwork up until then."

"So she was angry. Did you get the feeling she knew something more than she was letting on?"

"Not so much then, but after the fact. Now that she's gone, now that I've spent the last day trying to put things together in my head. Maybe she knew more than she wanted me to know. That would explain why she was so furious. I swear to you, I had no reason to hurt her. No matter how angry she was." He shrugged. "If anything, the way she was acting, I would've been the one who ended up floating in the bay. Anything to punish me for having the audacity to ask questions."

Was he telling the truth? Sure, I wanted to believe this

story, but that didn't mean he was being honest. I had to take off my daughter hat and put on my sleuth hat. Darn it, I had just put it on a high shelf in the closet in the hopes of never having to put it on again. There hadn't even been time for it to get dusty.

"So you really weren't seeing anybody else." That was one thing I absolutely had to confirm for Mom's sake. It was all she cared about, since she wouldn't allow herself to believe him capable of murder.

"Absolutely not. I was telling the truth when I assured your mother there was no one else in my life. There hasn't been for a while now." He lowered his voice. "How is she doing?"

I tried not to soften at the sound of real concern coming from him. He was still a murder suspect, and still someone who might end up breaking Mom's heart. "Like I said, she was upset. Though to be honest, she was more upset over the idea of you seeing someone else, since she doesn't believe for a minute that you're guilty." There couldn't be any harm in telling him that, could there? I sure hoped not.

Sheer relief spread over his face, the muscles sagging a little and making him look like a man closer to his actual age. "Thank goodness. I might actually get some sleep tonight, knowing that."

"I hate to tell you, but she's not the only person you need to be concerned about. You might know you didn't do this, but there's no evidence that anyone else did."

He waved this off like it didn't matter a bit. "I know once the police start digging into Moira's circle of friends and acquaintances, they'll find something. After all, it had to be one of them. From what the detective told me, her purse was on the dock. She wasn't even robbed. Doesn't it sound like this was someone she knew?"

I really did not want to agree with him. I really, really didn't. Not that I wanted him to be a murderer, but I didn't want to align myself with him too quickly. There was still plenty of opportunity for him to be the one who ended Moira's life.

But gosh darn it, he was so sincere. "I really couldn't say," I murmured, hedging my bets.

"Do you think I could call your mom?" he asked. Darned if he didn't bite his lip a little, like he feared the answer would be no.

All of my protective instincts bubbled up to the surface. My knee-jerk reaction would've been to warn against it. Mom didn't need this sort of complication in her life. It might've been better for her in the long run to move on before things got any more complicated.

But she liked him so much, and there were so many hours in which anybody in the whole wide world could've killed that woman. It didn't have to be him.

Even more than that, he had a gentle way about him. I doubted he was capable of murder, even though I knew anything was possible.

"Yeah, give her a call," I decided.

His smile was like sunshine breaking through storm clouds. I had made the right decision.

I hoped.

"Thank you so much. I know this will all work out in the end. I'm innocent, it just has to work out."

Poor, deluded guy. I didn't have it in me to remind him that things didn't always work out. I didn't want to kick him when he was already down.

"I really hope it does," I managed to reply over the lump in my throat.

And I was determined to see that it did work out, more for Mom's sake than for his.

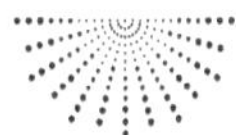

CHAPTER SEVEN

"What do you think of him?" I asked my father, standing beside him in front of the grill. The aroma was mouthwatering. He'd just thrown three sizable steaks on the grates, while foil-wrapped corn and potatoes were waiting to be removed and devoured.

After cooling off, unless I wanted to burn my mouth. I still hadn't quite learned to wait for my food to cool down before trying to eat. I was going to be such a great big sister.

He shrugged slightly. "To be honest with you, I've sort of let Joe run point on this case."

"How come?"

He lowered his brow, as well as his voice. "Emma. The main suspect is dating my ex-wife. How would that look?"

There went my foot, falling out of my mouth again. I wondered if there was a way to strap it in place. "Okay, sure. I wasn't thinking."

"Anyway, I have my own work to take care of. We might not get a lot of murderers in Cape Hope, but there is work to be done." And didn't I know it. That work had kept him constantly on the move throughout my childhood and adolescence.

"I know, I know. I just figured since Joe is the new kid, you might not want to give him such an important case."

"He's not a new cop, though. He has plenty of experience, and I have plenty of faith in him. Besides," he added, brushing melted butter and herbs on top of the meat, "it'll look good when he solves this. This could be good for his career."

That hardly instilled me with a sense of confidence. "Dad, please don't tell me you're trying to maneuver him into staying in Cape hope."

"What would be so bad about that?"

"For one thing, he's not sure he even wants to do it."

"Oh? You two have discussed this already?"

"In vague terms, yes. Nothing specific. But when I just casually brought up the idea of him being around so you could back off a little bit and maybe ease up your workload, he shut up like a clam. I felt like I said something wrong."

"Well, maybe he doesn't want to feel pressured into making a decision right away. He's only a month into this, and he signed on for at least half a year."

"You're right, you're right." Still, there was my father, trying to help him advance his career like he was a member of the family.

I knew him, no matter how he tried to play cute with me. He wanted Joe to be a member of the family. He'd always wanted me to marry a cop, though part of me couldn't imagine why. He knew all too well what it was like, a cop's life. Even in a quiet town like Cape Hope, it wasn't easy.

In fact, it might even have been more difficult in some ways. Wherever my father went, regardless of whether he was on duty or not, people came to him with their problems. They dragged him into their petty squabbles, like the big hullabaloo over a broken picket fence and ruined roses. Many was the time he'd stopped down at the store for a quart of milk or a loaf of bread and not come home for an hour, simply because he'd had the bad luck of being nearby when a fender bender took place.

Still, to him, my being involved with a cop would give him much less to worry about. Especially a cop he seemed to like as much as he liked Joe. If he helped make Joe a star on the Cape Hope force, so much the better.

"Did you get to meet Bob at all? Were you there when Joe questioned him?" I pulled the corn and potatoes off the grill with a pair of tongs and placed them on a platter while he flipped the meat. Was there anything sweeter than the sizzle of meat hitting a hot grill?

We both smiled, satisfied. Like father, like daughter.

His smile didn't last long, unfortunately. That gruff tone entered his voice again. "Sure, I saw him. I did a little digging into this Moira Banks and her past. That's been my contribution, limited though it is."

"Oh?" My nerves tingled. "What did you find out?"

"She was a real piece of work, that one. I don't think she had a single, actual friend."

"What makes you say that?" Granted, it fit with the sort of things Bob described, but I wanted to hear it from him.

"No matter who I or any of the officers have spoken to, it's always been the same. They served on committees together or knew each other socially, but weren't close. A few of them described her as the sort of person who didn't make friends easily. Someone who made herself difficult to know well. She kept people at arm's length. Unless she needed something from them—oh, yes," he added when my brows lifted practically straight off my head. "At least three people have made comments like that."

"She sounds like a real peach."

"You, my daughter, are far more diplomatic than I could ever be."

"Which isn't saying much, since I'm not generally a very diplomatic person."

He chuckled. "I hate to say it, but solving this case is going to be a real challenge." He plated the steaks, and I walked with him through the kitchen door.

Holly was inside, fixing up a salad. She had started to show a little and looked cute as anything standing at the counter, whisking salad dressing. "There you go again, talking about murder. For once, could we have a nice, pleasant conversation?"

"You make it sound like that's all we ever talk about," Dad countered in a gentle voice. It was very sweet, the way he toned himself down around her now. "Besides, Emma was the one who started the conversation down that road."

"Oh, sure! Throw me under the bus!" I rolled my eyes at Holly, and she laughed.

"But you did," Dad reminded me.

"Sure, I did. A crime has been committed, and for one reason or another, I care a lot about who did it and why."

"Just be sure you don't get too involved," he advised, putting more butter on the steaks before tenting them with foil so they could rest for a few minutes. The smell was killing me. I hadn't eaten lunch and was half starved.

"Do you ever get tired of saying the same things over and over?" I asked.

"Yeah, now that you mention it. And if you'd ever follow my advice, I wouldn't have to keep repeating myself."

I scowled. "You're lucky you know how to grill a good steak."

The little dog dancing around my ankles seemed to share my opinion. "If you think you're going to get a bite of that, you are sadly mistaken," I informed her, bending down to pet her head. "I love you, but not enough to give you any of my steak."

"I'd never seen a dog give somebody a dirty look before meeting her," Holly giggled.

"Yeah, just my luck. I got the dog with an attitude." I turned back to my father. "The only reason I'm involved with any of this is because of Mom, and you know it."

He looked deeply uncomfortable as he nodded. "I know that, and I hate to think of her dragging you into this. You already do enough damage on your own, you don't need anybody encouraging you to take risks."

"Oh, for heaven's sake." It was rare that I got good and annoyed with my father, but when I did it could get ugly. For a second, I wanted to remind him that it was very easy for him to take that attitude when he was living in domestic bliss with his girlfriend. His pregnant girlfriend. His pregnant, younger girlfriend.

Meanwhile, there was my mother, trying as best she could to put her life back together. All I wanted to do was help her with that, and he had nothing but scowls and gruff advice.

"All right, let's not argue." Holly placed the salad on the table. "It isn't worth it."

But I couldn't help myself. "What makes this a murder investigation, versus a suspicious death or something?"

I could tell he didn't want to continue, especially with Holly giving him a warning look. "She didn't drown. She was strangled by a scarf still knotted around her neck when the team pulled her out of the water."

"And her purse was found on the dock," I mused aloud, chomping on a slice of cucumber that only whetted my appetite more than ever. My taste buds revolted, wondering what business I had feeding them a cucumber when the scent of grilled meat filled the air.

"Right. Her wallet was full of cash and credit cards. It didn't even look like it had been touched, though it was dusted for fingerprints."

In spite of herself, Holly looked intrigued. "You mean to say a woman's purse sat out on the dock, out in the open, and nobody thought twice about it? Nobody noticed it?"

"There were old crates stacked at the far end and along the sides," Dad explained. "If it had been empty, sure, I can see your point. But the average person passing by wouldn't have noticed it."

"Strangulation. That's not the sort of thing a casual

acquaintance does, is it?" I asked. It wasn't really a question, and I didn't expect an answer.

Still, Dad gave me one. "Correct. Whoever killed that woman had a very personal reason to do so. This isn't like a shooting or stabbing, which is still more personal. And it wasn't accidental. She wasn't pushed, she didn't hit her head."

I got the feeling he was trying to send me a message without coming straight out and saying what was on his mind. He must've known by this point that Bob and Moira had a relationship at some point. He was trying to tell me that the nature of Moira's death pointed to Bob as a suspect.

No wonder he saw fit to avoid working the case. He clearly believed Bob did it, or at least wanted to believe he did. It wasn't like him to jump to conclusions about a suspect At least, I wasn't aware of him ever doing that. I'd always looked up to him as an example of a solid, honest detective who waited until all of the facts came in before he formed an opinion.

It seemed like just when I thought this couldn't get any more uncomfortable, I was proven wrong.

"I really wanted the job of decorating her house a few years back," Holly admitted. "It was after her husband died. She redid the entire place from top to bottom. Oh, I was practically salivating over the chance to take on a big job like hers. But she decided to go in another direction. Honestly, I was glad she did once I heard how difficult she was to work with."

"Oh, really?" I asked, sitting down to eat.

She joined me, sitting across the table. "Nothing was

ever good enough. She demanded things that weren't included in the original statement of work, which of course she'd agreed to and signed. The decorator who did the work ended up feeling cheated when it was all said and done, like she lost money because she devoted so much time to Moira's home when she could have been working on other projects. It was a very bitter experience in the end."

"It's a good thing you weren't involved. Everything works out the way it's supposed to," I murmured, lost in thought. So Moira was a difficult person, to put it mildly. She was also the sort who left people feeling cheated. The decorator, even Bob.

I turned to Dad. "When I talked to him, he said something about a fund he'd invested in when her husband was alive. That was how they originally knew each other, through business. He said—"

"I know what he said," Dad cut me off with a stern look. "And I don't like the idea of you questioning a suspect."

"I wasn't questioning him! I went to his house to talk to him as a favor to Mom."

"Since when can your mother not handle things like this on her own?"

"Can we please not argue about this?" Holly asked, looking from one of us to the other.

"I don't want to argue about it," I muttered while buttering my potato. I might have been pouting. It was all a blur.

"Maybe we should stop talking about it altogether since we can't seem to discuss this without tension." I could tell that one wasn't directed at me, even if I wasn't looking up from my plate. She was talking to my father, who only grunted in reply.

It was a funny thing. For all these years, he'd done his best to avoid Mom. Sure, they shared daughters, but we were adults. There weren't many group events in our lives anymore, like graduations or that sort of thing where they had to be together.

He'd felt free to move on, and he had done so without much delay. Now, his relationship with Holly was more serious than ever, thanks to the baby.

Still, I couldn't help but wonder if he took it personally, the fact that Mom was dating again. It was all fine and cool when she lived like a nun, not seeing anybody, without a social life aside from Trixie and Nell and her book club.

Now, she was showing him she'd moved on. It was okay for him to move on, but not for her.

"So, how are you feeling?" I asked Holly as a way of changing the topic. We didn't touch on Bob or the murder again.

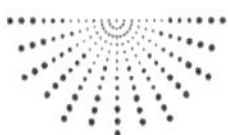

CHAPTER EIGHT

"I don't like the looks of her." Mom exchanged a glance with me before returning her attention to her tablet, where an image of Moira Banks filled the screen. "I know she's dead, and it's not right to speak ill of the dead, but she doesn't look like a very nice person."

"How can you tell just by looking at a picture?" Granted, from what I'd heard of her, I wasn't too impressed, either.

There she was, in all her glory, posed for a photo during some event or other. She wore a strapless dress that showed off her toned body and a deep tan, which set off her sun-bleached blond hair.

Her smile was hard. So were her eyes. Like she was trying to look happy.

Maybe I was reading too much into it. It was easy to do that now that I knew that slender neck had a scarf knotted around it when her body was found.

"At least I'm a natural blond," Mom whispered. I

wondered if she knew I heard her. Even in this dire situation, I had to hide a grin.

"How did Bob sound when you talked with him?" I asked, going back to frosting cupcakes. It was unusual for her to lose focus when there was so much work to be done, and somebody had to pick up the slack.

"Not as worried as I'd expected," she replied. "I was glad to hear it. I think he was more worried about my opinion on the situation."

"That's the feeling I got, too."

"Anyway, he's convinced the police will find the real killer and he'll be able to get back to his life without a murder hanging over his head."

I noted the quaver in her voice. "You don't share that opinion? About the police?" It took effort, hiding my curiosity. If there was one thing I knew about my mother, it was how much easier it was to get information out of her by asking casual questions. If I pressed for more, she'd shut down and remind me of my place in the relationship hierarchy.

Beneath her, in other words. She was the mother and she set down the rules.

"I don't know," she admitted. "Not that I don't have faith in Joe or even your father—" she said that word like it soured in her mouth, "—but there are always chances for situations like this to go wrong. If the police are set on him being the murderer, there's a chance they won't look at all options."

"I think you can trust Joe," I assured her, even as I hoped

I wasn't getting her hopes up for no reason. "He doesn't cut corners when he investigates."

"No, but you said it yourself back when he was investigating that murder case, when you met, that once he was set on something he stayed set on it."

"That's true." The more she talked, the more I wanted to shove an entire cupcake into my mouth. Anything to quell my rising anxiety. "It doesn't have to be that way, though."

"Just my luck." She leaned against the prep table, arms folded. "I decide to put myself out there, and something like this happens."

"Now I know where I get it from."

"Get what from?"

"My uncanny ability to draw drama into my life." I licked the offset spatula before tossing it into the sink. Even a tiny hit of sugar was better than nothing.

"I suppose it's genetic," she agreed with a sigh before going out to answer a knock at the door. I knew who it was, since he'd offered to stop by in the morning before the place opened. All the better to have a conversation without half the town being privy to every word.

Part of me wondered what would happen if I hung out in the kitchen and left Joe to answer Mom's plaintive questions. I was tempted to stay back there and listen by the door.

Then again, he'd already suffered through enough embarrassment at her house. And since that was all my idea, and since he'd warned me it was a terrible one, I figured I should just be nice and relieve him.

"Anybody for cupcakes?" I asked, carrying the tray out to the counter.

"Gee, I don't know. I was planning on having cupcakes for lunch and wouldn't want to spoil it." He rolled his eyes, even though a sigh of relief told me he was glad I'd joined them.

Why did he have to be so handsome? I found it difficult to take my eyes away from him long enough to stock the case with what I had just frosted. Which was saying something, since I normally paid way too much attention to cupcakes in general. Had the impossible happened? Had I finally met someone who I found more interesting than a sugary baked good?

Even Deke Bellingham would've come second to a freshly frosted cupcake, and that was saying something considering the fact that he was the best kisser I'd ever met.

"Didn't I tell you she spoke with Bob?" Mom asked, completely ignoring our banter. That was another miracle for the morning. Normally, she would've latched onto the fact that we playfully teased each other and turned it into something involving wedding bells.

All it had taken was meeting a man of her own to distract her from my personal life.

Granted, it helped that the man in question happened to be suspect in a murder investigation. Maybe one of the most morbid thoughts I'd ever had.

"She did," Joe confirmed, turning his attention back to her. "And I think that should be the last time she visits him privately, especially in connection with the case."

I made a face at the back of his head. "Um, hello? Could

you not talk about me like I'm not standing right here? Now I know how Lola feels."

"I'm sorry, did you hear something?" Joe asked, looking around like he had no idea who was talking. I couldn't decide if I wanted to eat a cupcake or throw it at him.

"Your nice work shirt would look so much better with frosting smeared all over the back," I observed.

"Try it and you buy it," he warned without turning around. "Along with buying me a new shirt for good measure."

"I'm serious. You know how much I adore somebody telling me what to do. I didn't know until now that I love it even more when they talk about me like I'm not here. If you don't knock it off with that, I'll leave and drive over to Bob's right now."

He turned slowly, sighing. "I wish I could say I thought you were kidding."

"I'm not kidding." I folded my arms, jerking my chin up. "Try me."

"Now, now, children. Let's not lose focus." Mom set about the task of taking the chairs down from on top of the tables, and Joe helped without being asked. Just when I wanted to waste a perfectly good cupcake and the cost of two dress shirts, he went and did something nice like that.

"Let me assure you, Mrs. Harmon—"

"Sylvia," she corrected. "I think you've earned the right to call me Sylvia."

"Have I?" I asked, stocking the bakery case again.

She ignored me. "Go on, please," she urged Joe.

"As I was saying, Sylvia, I can assure you that we're

looking at all possible leads. We've managed to piece together Moira's day based on what we found in her planner, at her home, and security footage from the businesses she visited that day. She had her hair done—"

Mom scoffed. "Bleached," she muttered. I snorted.

"—and had lunch with a friend before doing some shopping. We have her on camera in the lobby of the store before she left, deep in conversation on her phone. Unfortunately, we haven't found her phone. It wasn't in her purse, it's not in the house, and all that's left is the assumption that it was in her pocket when she went into the water. It might have fallen out at some point. We've arranged for divers to drag the bay for it."

And even if they found it in the water, it would be useless. There went that potential lead. If she was having a serious conversation, it might have meant she was fighting with somebody.

"By the way," he added for Mom's benefit, "we already checked Bob's phone. It wasn't him she was talking to. Though she reached out to him a while after that, and according to him that was when she asked him to meet with her."

"She asked him?" I stopped what I was doing, puzzled. "He made it sound like he was the one who wanted to talk to her."

"He told me about that, too," Mom piped up. "Maybe she got word of him being unhappy. He did tell me he was trying to reach somebody related to the fund for ages."

"Yes, that holds up. He forwarded me several messages he sent to her associates, with her cc'd on them. So his motive for meeting with her holds up." Joe patted Mom's arm with what I could tell was his attempt at a reassuring smile. "He's been extremely forthcoming and very helpful. All of that will work in his favor."

"Work in his favor?" she asked, her eyes darting back and forth over his face.

Uh-oh. I could tell from the way he tensed up that he saw his mistake, though it wasn't really a mistake. He was only trying to be honest with her, and part of that meant reminding her that the man was, indeed, suspect in a murder investigation. "I mean, when push comes to shove and the investigation progresses, it'll look good for him. The fact that he's being so helpful, that he's not holding anything back."

That wasn't good enough, not by a long shot. I felt sorry for him, so I jumped in. "Mom, let's be real. They're not going to stop looking at Bob as a suspect just because he says he didn't do it. Unfortunately, that's not how it works."

"And you know so much," she retorted.

My eyes widened. She wasn't usually like that with me, or with anybody for that matter. This whole situation was revealing a side of my mother that I wasn't sure I felt comfortable with. She was normally so gentle, soft-spoken for the most part. Sure, underneath she was tough as nails. I'd always known that, too.

It was just that the tough as nails part normally didn't show when she was talking to me.

I could tell Joe was getting more uncomfortable by the minute.

"Emma does make a good point. Believe me, the last

thing in the world I want is to discourage you in any way. I'm on your side, just like I'm on Bob's side. Unfortunately, this isn't entirely up to me. It's up to the prosecutor and judge and the jury—"

I wasn't the only one who had a habit of letting my foot fall out of my mouth. Once he started talking, he had a problem stopping.

Mom reeled like he'd struck her. "You really don't think it will come to that, do you?"

"Sylvia, I wish I could say it wouldn't. I want to say it wouldn't. But I just don't know. There's a line between hoping and being realistic. I know, you don't want to hear this," he said, frowning. "But we do have to be realistic. That doesn't mean we can't work hard to solve this in Bob's favor, but it does mean we cannot blindly get our hopes up and keep them there. I've been doing this for a long time. And honestly, if I could prove that every nice person was innocent, I would. It isn't always that simple. I wish it was."

The slightly defeated note in his voice made me sad for him. He cared so much about his job and about the people he served. It couldn't always turn out well, and he hated that.

For what it was worth, I hated it for him.

I also hated it for my mother, who now looked lower than I'd seen her in days.

"I understand." She sighed, shoulders sagging. She then turned to me, and it was like somebody had flipped a switch. She was determined, relentlessly so. "We'll just have to find out who really did it, then."

"Mom…" I looked at Joe and wasn't surprised to find him scowling. Of course, he would hate this idea.

Not like she cared. "Come on. You're good at this. You've done it before."

"I know, but aren't you the one who's always telling me not to get wrapped up in things like this?" Again, I glanced at Joe, torn between wanting to apologize and wanting to show him that it wasn't really my fault, my stubbornness and my inability to turn away from a problem. I'd got it from my mother just like I got it from my father. Genetically, I didn't have a prayer.

"And you too, of course," she continued, pleading with Joe. "Please. Don't settle on him as the killer. I just know it has to be someone else. I understand you have a job to do, and if you don't have the time to follow up on all the leads, maybe Emma can help you."

"Nothing like being volunteered for a job like this," I grumbled. I shrugged when Joe turned to me. *See what I deal with?* I asked silently.

He squeezed his eyes shut, wincing like he had a headache coming on. "Remind me again why I left Paradise City? Wasn't it to avoid things like this?"

"Here." I reached over the counter and handed him a cupcake. "I feel like you need this."

"Only one?" he muttered, taking it.

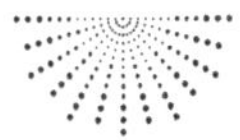

CHAPTER NINE

"So what's it like there? Is it just like *Casablanca*?"

Deke's laughter was like music to my ears after so much talk of murder and lies, even though he was thousands of miles away. "For one thing, *Casablanca* took place during World War II. Quite a lot of things have changed since then. For another thing, you really should try to make it out here yourself. I know you would love it. It's absolutely gorgeous."

I slumped back on the sofa, closing my eyes and trying to imagine the sort of things Deke was experiencing in Morocco. "You really do get the best assignments," I grumbled.

"Hey, you know there's plenty of chances for you to travel."

"Yeah, and now that Lola's cast is off, I won't feel so bad leaving her behind."

"There you go. Make sure to remind Marsha that you're available." Yes, our editor had promised to throw a few interesting jobs my way once I was available to travel further than the continental United States. I'd made a decision that I would start accepting those assignments, since I couldn't stick around for the sake of my family.

Then again, there I was, worried about Mom. Though Deke had a special talent for improving my mood—which hadn't always been the case, not by a long shot—I couldn't keep my thoughts from returning to Mom and Bob and an unfortunate murder.

"Did I tell you Mom started dating? I mean, it's been a while, but we haven't exactly been on the same schedule, you and me."

"That's great! I'm glad for her. It's about time she got back out there. How's it going?" Then, he chuckled knowingly. "Let me guess. She's driving you nuts."

"You have no idea just how right you are," I groaned. That was when I told him what was going on. At least, the abridged version. Bob, his dead ex, the fact that he happened to see her earlier the same evening she was probably murdered.

"What is it about you, Harmon?" he asked. I could just imagine him shaking his head, sitting in some fabulous location, wearing his uniform of jeans and a button-down shirt.

And a know-it-all smirk. He tended to wear that a lot, too, at least when he was around me.

"What's that supposed to mean?" I asked.

"You know exactly what it means. Even when you try, you can't keep yourself away from situations like this."

"I will have you know that it's been weeks and weeks

since I was involved in a murder investigation, thank you very much. The situation with Charlie had nothing to do with murder, in case you forgot."

"How could I forget? I was so relieved nobody would be pulling a gun on you."

"There you go. How can I help what happens around me? Especially when, for the first time ever, my mother is actively urging me to find a way to help solve the mystery. Normally, she's the one telling me to play it safe and mind my own business."

"She must have a lot of faith in this guy."

I remembered the way she smiled when he walked into the café, how she'd hummed to herself as she got ready to see him. How gooey they were over each other. "She does," I agreed.

"What about you? What you think about him?"

"That's a loaded question."

He chuckled. "How so?"

"I mean, he clearly likes Mom, and she likes him a lot. A whole lot. Like, it's almost embarrassing to see the two of them together. It's like they're thirteen years old and just discovering the opposite sex."

"Not a mental image I felt like entertaining today…"

"Then you really don't want to know what she confessed when Joe questioned her about what she and Bob were doing the night of the murder." Just thinking about it made me gag in my mouth a little.

He laughed. "No, but thank you for putting that thought in my head. You still haven't told me how you feel about him, though. You told me what your mom thinks and how he feels about her. What do you think? What do your instincts tell you?"

"Wow, you sound like you put any kind of faith in my instincts at all," I teased.

"I do. You know I do. All kidding aside, you are generally on the money when it comes to what's in a person's heart. I scoffed originally, I admit that, but you've proven yourself."

"I didn't know that was what I was doing," I chuckled. Lola jumped up in my lap, the little attention hog, and I absentmindedly petted her while considering the question. "I believe him. I do. I don't think he killed her. I'm sure this is just a misunderstanding. I mean, it's worse than that for the woman who's dead now, but you know what I mean. He met with her and left her and went out with Mom and that was it."

I told myself not to think about what happened between nine o'clock and two-thirty, but it was impossible. My mind liked to torture me with things like that.

"Then that's good enough for me. I trust your judgment. So, let me guess. Mom wants you to help clear his name."

"Boy, you sure are insightful."

"No, I've just known you long enough to know how these things generally turn out. And you'll do it, too. You'll find a way."

"To be honest, I don't know if I can on this one."

"That isn't like you, sounding so defeated this early in the game. What's the challenge?"

"For one thing, there's no proof that he didn't do it. He showed up at Lou's around seven o'clock, just like he was supposed to. But there's no way for him to prove where he was between the time he was with Moira and the time he arrived at the restaurant. The witnesses who saw the two of them talking all say it was around six. That gives him a solid hour."

"Yeah, but what was he going to do? Kill her in broad daylight? That must have been what happened. I mean, if he was the one who did it. Unless he took her someplace else, killed her there, then dumped her body. But why would he do it in the same vicinity where he was last seen with her? It doesn't make sense."

"I know it doesn't, and I'm sure Joe knows it, too."

As soon as I said his name, I wished I hadn't. While the iciness between the two men had seemed to thaw out by the time Deke left town, I still felt like it was a touchy subject. Deke and I weren't seriously involved, nor had we ever been, but he had taken it very personally when he found Joe visiting Cape Hope at the same time he was.

Joe had taken it personally, too, leaving me in the middle. It was a lot of fun.

"I have all the faith in the world in him," he finally admitted. I knew it took a lot for him to say that, which made me smile.

"That's all fine and good, but unless we can find out where Moira went after she met up with him, this is all for nothing. He'll be the last person seen with her, and he'll be the one everybody thinks is the killer."

"Something tells me a woman like her had more than one person wanting to strangle her."

Of course! Sometimes I forgot Deke had a history with

people like Moira and her late husband. "Did you know her? I didn't even think to ask."

"Not personally. I think my father did business with her husband back in the day; the name is familiar. From what I remember of her, she was the same as so many others."

"And what does that mean?"

"Money hungry. Obsessed with wealth, status. Always trying to outdo somebody else. I'm surprised you never saw her around."

"Oh, sure. Because I run in those sort of circles. Between charity functions and driving around town in my Lexus, I hardly have time to find a new staff to run my mansion."

"Okay, okay."

I got serious then. "She didn't live anywhere near Cape Hope, anyway. I'm sure she came down to meet with Bob especially, since he was being a bit of a squeaky wheel over lack of communication with the fund. I don't know anything about that sort of stuff," I admitted, though I was sure it wasn't a secret.

"Anyway, she probably wasn't much fun as a person. I remember hearing something about one of her ex house-keepers complaining that she was a real shrew."

"I'm sure the list of people who had problems with her is endless," I admitted. "Unless I can narrow that list down to one person, it doesn't really matter. Does it?"

"You'll find a way. You always do." Then, he got quiet for a second before adding, "You know, if she was still involved with that fund, and the fund was started by her husband, there's another angle to the situation which the police might not have put together yet."

I sat up so fast, Lola almost fell off my lap to the floor. And the thing was, I normally would've fallen all over myself trying to apologize to her, but right then I was far too interested in what Deke had suggested. "What? What is it?"

"There's another thing I remember about that Banks guy. I remember my father talking about him once; he wouldn't get involved in any of his funds, or anything he was involved with in any way. It's funny, too, because Banks was always so successful. It was a practically guaranteed return on the investment. He refused. He was steadfast."

"Why?"

"For one thing, he was always insistent that there was no such thing as a surefire moneymaker. He always found it strange that these investors bragged over how much money they'd made. And how they'd lost absolutely nothing. It seemed to him that the law of averages meant everybody had to experience a failure at least once. But not this Banks guy. Everything he touched turned to gold."

"A Ponzi scheme?" I whispered, breathless. I had learned all about those during the big scandals from the past decade or so. So many people had lost their life savings, dazzled by the chance of a sure thing.

"He insinuated there was something else going on. That some of the investors in these funds were shady guys. He didn't want to have anything to do with people like that. I never saw any proof of these bad guys being involved."

"Maybe I'll have to do a little looking into it myself," I mused.

"Hang on a second," he was quick to protest. "I wouldn't move so fast if I were you."

"Why not?" I asked in a voice that sounded suspiciously like I was whining. "Don't get me all excited and then tell me to hold off."

"I'm sitting here half a world away, warning you that this dead man might've had business dealings with shady characters, and you wonder why I want you to take it easy? Come on, think about it."

"You know, it always excites me so much when you get all sarcastic with me," I muttered.

"I mean it," he insisted rather than taking the bait. "Give the tip to Joe or your father or to whoever you want but stay out of that part of it. It's not worth risking your neck."

"Okay, okay," I grumbled.

"That's not very convincing."

"Maybe I wasn't trying to convince you," I retorted.

"And that comes as such a surprise," he replied. I couldn't see him. I wished I could, really I did, since he was terribly easy on the eyes, but I could hear a smirk in his voice.

"You're lucky you're not here so I can threaten to slap you."

"Yet another thing that would come as no surprise." He laughed.

CHAPTER TEN

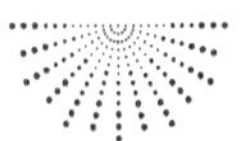

"What's wrong?"

I looked at my father, wide-eyed and innocent. "What do you mean?"

"What do you mean, what do I mean? You never visit me here." He looked down at the spread I'd left on his desk. "And you don't come bearing food."

"I thought maybe you could use something to eat. And if you don't want it, maybe somebody else around here will." I sniffed a little, offended, if only jokingly. "That's the last time I ever make up a basket for you."

He looked over the lemon bars, carrot cake muffins, snickerdoodles, and cranberry scones. "Did you get any sleep last night at all?"

"Please, you know I could bake blue-ribbon treats while wearing a blindfold and half-asleep."

"Please," he groaned, rubbing his temples. "Don't even joke about using the oven when you aren't fully awake."

"You know I wouldn't do that." I sighed. "But I did want to bring you something."

"You brought enough for the entire station."

"Good! I hope everybody enjoys it." I perched on the edge of his desk, arms folded. He always kept a clean, neat desk. Not like some of the other ones around, covered in stacks of paper and empty coffee cups.

He only kept a few photos on his desk, too. One of Darcy and me together, and one of him and Holly. Before long, they would be joined by a picture of the new baby.

It had been over a month, yet the thought of being a big sister was still so strange. I'd been a little sister my entire life.

"What brings you here?" He eyed me up in a way only a parent could. "Come on. Fess up."

I sighed. "Well, obviously, I want to see how things are going down here."

He wasn't impressed. "With the Moira Banks case, you mean."

"Yes, Dad. That's what I mean." The man was exhausting. I dropped the sweet act. "I wanna know what's going on with it. Jeez."

"You're really set on digging into this, aren't you? Did your mother put you up to coming down here?"

I bristled but did what I could to keep my temper in check. We rarely discussed Mom, and now I remembered why. His attitude was a little much when he mentioned her. Sarcastic.

"Maybe she didn't have to," I informed him. "Maybe I want to do this for her because I know how much it means."

I could tell he was annoyed, which annoyed me. I was annoyed with myself, too, for assuming everything was hunky-dory when it came to his feelings toward her. Silly me had figured that once he moved on to Holly and built a life with her, he wouldn't mind seeing my mother move on with her life. I'd also hope time had smoothed over any sharp edges left over from their divorce.

Silly me.

"This is a pretty big ask," he muttered.

"It isn't so big. If Bob didn't commit murder, there is no reason why I shouldn't try to help clear his name. Or would you rather see the wrong person go to jail for this?"

"You know I wouldn't."

"But you would prefer the innocent man not also being the man Mom is dating. Right?"

"I really don't think I need to get into this with you, young lady." Oh, he sounded so insufferably like a father just then. I almost pitied my unborn sibling when he talked that way.

"Would you just admit that it bothers you? Seriously. I'm a grown-up, I can handle it."

"This is not the time or the place." He looked around, barely whispering as he chided me. Like heaven forbid anybody overhear us having a conversation.

I whispered right back, leaning in to make sure he heard me. "I didn't hear you complaining that I was sticking my nose into things when I asked Holly to have lunch with me after news of the baby spread. You didn't seem to have problem with that, even though anybody who's spent more than five minutes in this town would know that I would be looked at like a traitor, like I was taking your side over Mom's. But that was okay, wasn't it?"

That was a mistake. I knew it even as I spoke. Patches of red bloomed on my father's cheeks as his jaw tightened. "You are dangerously close to the line, Emma Jane," he warned. Oh, how many times had I heard him talk that way? Probably more than I should've been comfortable with, since it meant I'd been driving him crazy my entire life.

"Dad, please. You see my point, I hope. I don't want to fight with you."

He didn't answer right away. instead, he reached into the basket, pulled out a lemon bar and took a huge bite. So that was where I'd inherited my penchant for eating my feelings.

"This is good," he mumbled with his mouth full, powdered sugar ringing his mouth.

"Thank you."

"Holly wouldn't love knowing I'm eating sweets, especially this early in the day."

"Then I'll make it a point not to tell her," I winked. Had I won the fight? I almost couldn't believe it. It was like seeing a unicorn standing under a double rainbow while a leprechaun danced around holding a pot of gold. Maybe the Loch Ness monster could make an appearance and really seal the deal.

"I still don't like you getting involved in this—no matter the reason why," he insisted, licking sugar off his fingers.

"I know. For the record, I'm not crazy about it, myself."

"So why do you allow yourself to get roped in? Can you tell me that? I've always wanted to know why. Certainly, my warnings fall on deaf ears. What drives you?"

"What drives you?" I countered, picking at a snickerdoodle. After chocolate chip cookies, they were probably my favorite. Especially when made with browned butter, which I had naturally used because I was a very fancy person.

"Come again?"

"Why do you do what you do? What made you become a cop? You know, I don't think I've ever asked you that."

"Not true. You used to ask me when you were little."

"I don't remember you answering."

"I probably didn't," he admitted, shamefaced. "It's not an easy question to answer. Catching bad guys. That's the most likely answer I would've given, but there's more to it than that. I don't know why, exactly. It's what I feel compelled to do."

"I feel compelled, too, and please don't roll your eyes," I begged.

"I didn't."

"You were going to."

"So what if I was? Emma, you're my daughter. Forgive me if I don't want my daughter doing work like this when she hasn't been trained to."

"I'm only asking questions and doing research. That's the most I ever do."

"Yet you find a way to get yourself in dangerous situations which you're completely unprepared for."

"But I always make it out, don't I?"

"Sorry if that doesn't instill confidence," he snickered. "But I tend to worry about my daughter getting herself in hot water, regardless of whether or not she happens to get lucky and find a way out of it."

"No hot water here. Lukewarm at best." I crossed my heart for the second time in the last two days.

"Sure, sure." He wiped his hands, then sighed. "Why did you really come in, besides wanting to raise my blood sugar and blood pressure in one fell swoop?"

I cracked my knuckles, ready for a fight. "Has anybody looked into the guys Moira's late husband did business with? Maybe they were clued into the same issues Bob had with the fund they were involved in. Maybe they wanted to know where their money went. Or maybe they knew exactly where it went, and they wanted to shut her up since she knew, too, and Bob was pressing her to find out why the returns stopped coming in."

"That's an interesting theory."

"Thank you."

"Which we're already looking into. I'm telling you, sweetheart," he chuckled when I couldn't help sighing in disappointment, "this is what we do. None of us is a first-timer here. We're all well aware of the steps to take in a case like this. And yes, Joe has already requested that the officers working with him look into everyone Nicholas Banks did business with."

"That's great!"

"It's a very, very long list," he continued. "I can't over-state how long."

"That's not so good."

"He was in business for decades, kiddo."

"Why not narrow it down to the people he was involved with over the last several years before he died? Yes, yes, I know," I groaned, holding my hands up. "You've already thought of that, too."

"Joe has," he assured me. "You don't give him enough credit."

"I give him plenty of credit," I muttered. It was he who didn't give me the credit I deserved.

"Then why not sit back and let the man do his job? I realize you don't see it this way, but cops are sort of funny about reacting to people telling them how to do their job. How would you feel if someone was always telling you they would write an article better than you did?"

I hated how right he was. "I guess I never thought of it that way."

"Listen." He leaned in a little, glancing around again to be sure we weren't overheard. God forbid anybody hear him being a father. "I think he really takes it to heart, the fact that this Bob Perlman is involved with your mom. For the record, I think it's great. I really do," he insisted when I maybe sort of smirked a little. "I want to see her move on with her life. No, it didn't work out between us, but that doesn't mean she's not a terrific lady. We did have a lot of happy years. I never wanted her to shut down after we split up."

"That's good to hear," I admitted.

"Anyway, I think he wants to make this right for her, and for you. And don't you dare tell him I said that," he warned.

My cheeks flushed painfully. "I don't want that. Now, don't get me wrong," I whispered, "I think he's great. I do. And I'm not saying that if things weren't right, we wouldn't maybe see where we could go together. But it isn't that simple."

"Why isn't it simple?" He grimaced in disbelief. "It seems pretty simple from where I sit."

"Isn't that nice for you," I teased, though I wasn't joking. My teasing was used to cover up how annoyed I was. "He hasn't walked down the easiest road."

"You mean his wife."

I practically had to hold my jaw in place to keep it from falling on the floor. "Yes, that's exactly what I mean. You knew about that?"

"You'd be surprised by the sort of conversations that happen around here during quiet times." He winked. "I think it's a terrible shame what happened. But, time has passed, and it takes a pretty special person to make a man want to move on after something like that. If you are that special person, so much the better. I wouldn't be a bit surprised."

"Please, let's not speculate," I begged. He wasn't doing my already conflicted feelings any favors by saying sweet things like that.

"Okay, fine. But my point remains. I think he wants to impress you, or at least show you he cares by helping your mom—and indirectly, helping you, since I'm sure she isn't making your life very easy."

"No comment," I muttered with a frown.

He chuckled gently. "So I suspected. At any rate, I say all this to say you don't have anything to worry about. He's going all-in on this."

"I know that's supposed to make me feel better, but I

worry about him, too. I don't want to see him getting stressed out again."

"Is it just me, or do you sound very concerned about him?" There was a fatherly twinkle in his eye.

"Maybe I am. I would be worried about Raina, too, if she was stressed out enough to have a panic attack that landed her in the emergency room." I stuck out my tongue when he rolled his eyes. "Well? It's true. Joe is my friend."

"You're impossible."

"I've heard that one before," I grinned before taking another snickerdoodle.

"Hey. I thought those were for us, here at the station." He nudged the basket away from me, closer to himself.

"Yeah? And I'm at the station right now, aren't I?" I winked before taking a big bite.

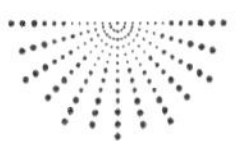

CHAPTER ELEVEN

"Be nice," Mom warned as we closed up for the night.

"Nice? Why wouldn't I be nice?"

"All right. Maybe that isn't the correct word. Gentle? Polite?"

I rolled my eyes and wiped the counter harder than I was before. "Since when am I not polite? Since when?"

"I know you don't intend to be impolite, but there are times when your mouth gets the better of you."

I shot her a withering look. "Wow. Have you ever looked in a mirror?"

"Emma Jane."

Wow. That was twice in the same day that one of my parents called me by my full name. I might as well have been ten years old again.

"Sylvia Elizabeth," I retorted, sticking out my tongue. "Okay. I'll keep from asking a million questions when Bob gets here."

"Which he is about to do." Mom smoothed out her

blouse and ran a hand over her hair. Sure enough, he was across the street and waiting for a car to pass before crossing.

"Do you know how breathless you get whenever you see him?" I giggled.

"Hush, young lady, or you will leave. You're only here because you promised to be on your best behavior."

"Okay, fine." I kept wiping the same spot as before.

Naturally, she noticed. "You're going to rub a hole." Even now, she couldn't refuse an opportunity to micromanage.

A second later, in came Bob. Her face lit up like a Christmas tree. So did his. I felt like I'd stepped into a romance novel. One that made me cringe a little and maybe even consider taking a shower with all my clothes on.

"Hi, Emma," Bob grinned. "I just had a long talk with your friend, Detective Sullivan."

"Oh?" I pointedly ignored Mom's knowing look. I didn't even have to glance her way to imagine it in my mind's eye. Should I have warned her to cool it with the Detective Joe stuff the way she'd warned me to be polite?

"He seems fond of you." Bob exchanged a little smile with my mother.

"Ugh. Mom." I shot her a dirty look. "Could you not air my laundry all over the place?"

She waved a hand. "I might've mentioned that you're good friends. What's so bad about that?"

I had to remind myself that I'd promised to be polite. Something told me that meant not killing her.

"I also ran into your father." Very telling, the way he

referred to Dad that way. Not as Mom's ex-husband. He didn't even look her way. "He speaks highly of you."

"Good to know." I chuckled.

He turned to Mom then. "And of you."

"You were talking about me?" She gasped, a hand over her chest. "What about?"

"Nothing in particular. I got the feeling he'd take me out to the woods and shoot me if I wasn't good to you, though. I can't imagine my ex-wife speaking so warmly about me."

Wait a second.

Ex-wife? I'd never heard anything about an ex-wife.

Judging by the sudden pale hue of Mom's cheeks—they'd just been flushed with excitement at seeing him—she hadn't heard about this, either.

The silence which fell over the café after that little slip of the tongue was profound. I could've heard a pin drop all the way back in the kitchen.

My stomach clenched, along with my heart. This was not the twist I'd seen coming. Of course, did anyone ever see a twist coming? Wasn't that what made it a twist in the first place?

Even in my head, I was babbling to myself. I had to do something, since the shock and panic and discomfort and awkwardness were too much to handle on their own.

Of course, nothing I was feeling touched what Mom was going through. Her eyelids fluttered to the point where I was afraid she was about to faint. I was poised, ready to catch her if that happened. She had me that convinced that she was about to go down.

She didn't. She was too strong for that. "Excuse me?" she

breathed, staring at Bob. "Your ex-wife? You never mentioned being married before."

He shrank under her glare. And when his eyes cut over in my direction, he didn't find a friend in me, either. If anything, I was angrier than she was. He hadn't told me about a wife, either, when we met up on his porch.

"It isn't that I wanted to hide her from you," he began, licking his lips more than seemed normal. It was clear he knew he was in trouble and was looking for a way out of the hole he'd just dug. "It's just that she never came up in conversation."

"Hold on." Mom's voice took on an edge I was starting to get used to; not that this was anything to be happy about. "I told you everything about my marriage. I mean, not everything. Not the specifics. But you at least knew I was once married. You knew I have two daughters. Oh, my goodness." She pressed a hand to her chest again, "Do you have children you didn't tell me about?"

"No! No, we never had children. Janice was always in delicate health, for one reason or another."

"Her name is Janice," Mom whispered, and I noticed she was swaying back and forth a little like she was standing on the deck of a ship during a storm. The poor woman was just trying to keep her balance in the midst of all this.

"Yes." He looked and sounded contrite. If he'd dropped to his knees and begged forgiveness, it wouldn't have come as a surprise. If anything, that was exactly what I wanted to see him do just then. It was the least he could do, really.

"How long were you married?" she asked. I touched her

arm to remind her she wasn't alone in this, and I hoped she knew without being told how upset I was for her sake.

It was no crime, having an ex-spouse. Why did he always feel like he had to keep things from her? I could imagine how betrayed she'd feel after already having suspected him of going behind her back with another woman. Now, this.

"Twenty-three years," he admitted. "We've been divorced for nearly eight. See, it isn't that I want to keep her a secret. I barely think about her anymore. We haven't been a part of each other's lives in so long."

"Do you pay alimony?" I had to know. A man who wrote a check to his ex every month could hardly forget about her.

"There was no need for that," he replied. To my surprise, he didn't sound irritated that I'd asked. He was too busy trying to make things right. "She has money of her own, and she didn't sue for it. Her lawyer wanted her to. I always thought he did, anyway. She refused."

"Good for her," I muttered. This guy was a real piece of work.

"Why didn't you tell me, anyway?" Mom asked. "Don't you see how this looks? Now, I'll always wonder what else you've kept secret."

"Sylvia, I swear, I didn't do it deliberately. I would've told you about her soon. I mean it," he insisted, and now he didn't sound plaintive or apologetic anymore. "I would've told you soon. Maybe on our next date, even, or the next time we talked on the phone. The whole situation with Janice has been fraught from the beginning."

"I thought you said you weren't part of each other's

lives," I countered, since it seemed my mother was having trouble keeping up.

"We aren't in the normal sense," he insisted. "If anything, the only reason I think of her at all or have any contact is because of the way she guilts me. We were never a healthy couple in any normal sense. I know that. I think I knew it for a long time. Our entire relationship was based on codependence. I learned that after going to therapy; I wanted to know why things didn't work out. You'd think after twenty-three years, a marriage would be stable enough to keep going."

He sank into one of the chairs with a defeated sigh. "This is not the way I imagined explaining this. I didn't want you to think I was… I don't know. Broken. Or a fool for staying with her as long as I did. That wasn't the impression I wanted you to have."

"No, you'd rather give me the impression of you being a liar."

"I didn't lie."

Good luck, buddy. I'd tried that one on her before, and she didn't let me get away with it, either. "You forgot to tell the truth, which is as good as lying."

I almost felt sorry for the guy. And almost wanted to tell him not to bother arguing the point, since she'd never give in. And even if she did, I wouldn't.

"Would you have looked at me the same way if I admitted on our first date that I stayed with my ex-wife because her health problems made me feel sorry for her? Because I didn't want to be the bad guy? Even when I had the suspicion that she was never quite as sick as she insisted she was? Or would I have looked callous? Or like a doormat who'd allowed himself to be used for more than twenty years?"

"I don't know," Mom admitted. "But you could've given me the chance to decide for myself, rather than assuming how I would've reacted."

Even so, her tone had already softened like she was starting to feel sorry for him. She made her way out from behind the counter and eventually settled into a chair across from where he sat. "What happened?" she asked, no longer sounding half as upset as she was just moments earlier.

"Hang on," I interjected, untying my apron. "Why don't I leave you guys to it? I don't need to be here for this." No matter how much I wanted to hear it.

Bob shook his head. "No, I want you to know. It means a lot that you see where I was coming from." How could I argue with that even if I wanted to?

Not that I wanted to.

He took a deep breath. "We were introduced by a mutual friend while we were both in our mid-twenties. She was an artist, which I found attractive; I was always the serious guy who had his mind on work, while she was a free spirit. We were married soon after. It was a whirlwind sort of thing, which made it seem even more romantic. Her health issues started roughly a year after the wedding."

"What sort of issues?" Mom asked. She was being way more diplomatic than I could ever have managed.

"Oh, you name it. Unexplained aches and pains. She'd wake up in the middle of the night and complain of short-ness of breath. I'd take her to the hospital. Or I'd wake to the sound of her crying out for help. She'd be at the bottom of the stairs, claiming she fell. I can't tell you how many times we ended up in the emergency room. Or how many times I had doctors and nurses ask questions pertaining to my role in her injuries."

"Was she injured?" I asked.

"No." He gave me a sick little smile. "No, she wasn't. She was rarely even bruised. If you don't believe me, I can provide medical records. I kept copies of absolutely everything after a while, in case I needed to prove at any point that nothing was really wrong with her."

It left me feeling sick to my stomach, and something told me he'd barely scratched the surface.

"Was she ever evaluated for some deeper illness? Aren't there people who pretend to be sick or even convince themselves they are?"

"Sure, and she was," he nodded. "But because this was so sporadic and because there was no proof of her causing anything herself, there was never an official diagnosis. This was a quarter of a century ago, mind you. Not the dark ages by any means, but we still know more now than doctors did back then. Before long, I decided she was doing this to get attention."

He looked at Mom. She was watching him intently.

He continued, "Which was why I was afraid you'd think I was callous. But here's the thing. I started drawing parallels between arguments we'd have or business trips I'd announce—visiting one of my stores, board meetings, what have you—and her spells. She'd take to her bed for three or four days before I left and stay there for a week after I returned. I was never sure whether or not she was serious. Maybe she was. I couldn't afford to dance to her tune, though. Literally, or else I'd have to give up the business. I couldn't be her full-time caregiver, and she refused to have help in the house."

He looked down at his hands, folded on the table.

I let out a silent breath. This was heavy stuff.

"It took twenty-three years for me to decide enough was enough. I'm ashamed of having taken so long to walk away. I didn't want to be the bad guy; I recognize that now. I knew she'd play up her illnesses and accuse me of not caring. I was even afraid she'd accuse me of harming her just to get back at me. Enough was finally enough, though. I just didn't care anymore. To my shock, she accepted the divorce and everything went smoothly. I found myself angry that I hadn't done it years earlier. I wasted so much time."

I didn't know what to think, not that it mattered. Mom's opinion mattered. Mom's feelings. She was unreadable, sitting stock-still and barely blinking or even breathing.

"I was wrong not to tell you, but how would I even begin to share that story?" he asked. "You have no idea how much I wanted to tell you everything. I want to share everything with you. But I didn't want to scare you off, either, or make you think she's still a presence in my life. She's not. I don't know—" He shrugged. "It seems I'm still the man who was too afraid to walk away. Even now, she has that power over me. And even now, she's finding a way to affect my life."

"Don't blame that on her," Mom warned. "You made this choice. Keeping her from me. That was you. You might need more therapy."

Ouch. I couldn't help feeling sorry for the guy. He looked defeated, slumping in the chair like he'd slumped on his porch when I went to talk to him. "You might be right."

"I think I need a little time to work through this," she admitted in a whisper. "I don't mean to break things off or anything like that. I just need time."

"I understand."

"Even if it seems like I'm abandoning you at the worst possible time?" she asked in a whisper even softer than before.

"You don't owe me anything," he reminded her with what I guessed was supposed to be a smile. "You really don't. I've already put you through enough."

Neither of us stopped him from leaving.

When he was gone, Mom's resolve finally broke. I watched with an aching heart as she lowered her head to her arms, folded on the table.

CHAPTER TWELVE

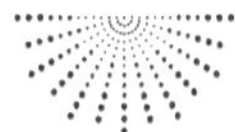

The sounds of frivolity and general summer joy surrounded me as I mopped grease off a fresh slice of pizza. Extra cheese, obviously, because I deserved it after the Mom debacle.

"What did you do?" Darcy asked, wide-eyed.

"What do you think? I finished closing up the café, made sure she got home all right, and called the two of you." I lifted the massive slice to my mouth, thanking the gods for the invention of such majestic deliciousness. Just the thing I needed after what I'd witnessed earlier.

All things considered, it was probably preferable to eat unhealthy foods when I was stressed out than it would be to drink or do drugs. This was what I told myself to rationalize my choices.

I couldn't help but notice the way Joe winced when I told the story, and how he still looked guilty as sin. "Don't tell me you knew about this," I warned.

He looked from me to Darcy and back again. "I didn't

know he never told her! It's not as if I was deliberately keeping information to myself. Besides, it's none of my business."

"You could have mentioned it to me."

"I'm not a gossip."

"It's not gossip if it was helping somebody not get their heart broken," he insisted.

"Do you really think her heart is broken?" Darcy asked, picking at her own slice as the three of us sat at the counter with our backs to the boardwalk. The kids working the pizza ovens were running around like chickens with their heads cut off to take care of the many guests wandering in and out of the store.

"Well, she's pretty upset. It doesn't look good, the fact that he neglected to mention an ex-wife. Pretty soon, she's going to start asking herself if she can trust him at all."

"Which means she's going to lose faith in him when it comes to the case," Joe concluded.

"That's what I'm afraid of," I admitted before taking another bite. The crust was nice and crispy, and the cheese was perfectly gooey. Yet not even a taste sensation like this could make me feel better.

"There are plenty of fish in the sea," Darcy concluded. "Is that what she told you after your breakup? And it's what she told me after I stopped seeing Karl." Her voice got softer toward the end there, and I knew she wasn't over him yet. They hadn't even been together for very long, but she was still tender on the subject.

"But he was the first big catch after a long time in an otherwise empty boat," I reminded her.

"That's a very strange analogy," Joe muttered.

"I don't remember asking for your opinion on it," I sniffed, then continued. "This isn't going to be easy to get over. In fact, it might be enough to make her retreat back into her shell, which is the last thing I want."

I expected Joe to disagree with me, since that was normally what he did. He was very good at it, too. Only he didn't, not this time. "Yeah, it takes a lot of guts to get back out there after a long time. She'll probably regret it, but hopefully it won't last forever. She has the two of you to help her through it, and her friends, which is a lot more than some people have."

Naturally, I knew exactly what he was talking about, and I felt sorrier for him than ever. He didn't have anybody to help him get past losing his wife, or getting back up on the horse—so to speak.

Darcy was clueless about that, of course, which was why she moved right past what he said without thinking twice. "We have his side of the story. I wonder what his wife's side of the story is."

"You have the same look on your face that you had when I borrowed your favorite sweater to wear on my first date with Jimmy O'Connor," I murmured, filled with dread.

"You mean, when you ruined my favorite sweater by spilling soda all over yourself like a clumsy idiot," she was quick to remind me.

"And you pushed me off the front porch, and I landed in the hedges, and you got grounded for two weeks," I concluded. "You had that same look on your face, like you wanted to murder somebody."

"Wow, it sounds like you two were a lot of fun when you were kids," Joe muttered before finishing one of the two slices he'd ordered. He liked white pizza versus the kind with red sauce, which made me seriously reevaluate our entire friendship. As far as I was concerned, pizza without sauce was just crust and cheese. Why not just advertise it as crust and cheese and stop lying?

Darcy ignored him; something she was getting better at the more time we spent together. "I don't want to murder him. But I am concerned, the same way you are. He's messing with our mom here."

"Can I remind you both that no one is messing with anybody?" Joe asked.

I almost felt sorry for him, sitting between us while we talked over and around him.

"What? Do you think it's cool that he didn't tell Mom he had an ex-wife?" she asked him.

"No, I know better than to tell either of you something you don't want to hear—and I don't think it's cool," he added when it looked like Darcy was about to start swinging. "No, it seems pretty sketchy. He isn't doing himself any favors when it comes to making himself out to be a sympathetic character. He becomes less trustworthy all the time."

He then turned to me. "You know how hard it is trying to stay objective when you tell me things like this?"

"Sorry," I murmured. The thing was, he was the first person I thought of calling after that scene in the café. Darcy had been an afterthought. I didn't know how I felt about that, but it was true.

"And I believe him," he continued, turning to Darcy. "He

didn't want to make himself out to be a bad guy, and he didn't know how to tell that story without sounding like he didn't care about his wife. Obviously, he did care, and she took advantage of him."

"That's how you see it?" I asked.

"What, are you going to threaten to punch me?" He folded his slice in half before taking a huge bite. At least his eating technique was on point.

"No, not at all. If anything, I agree with you."

"You what?" Darcy asked, eyes bulging.

"Is that how I look when I can't believe something you said?" I asked Joe, nodding to her.

"Yeah, the two of you really do look alike."

"I mean it," I told her. "That was a touchy conversation. Yes, he could've told her he used to be married. He didn't need to tell her the entire backstory. That could've waited until they were dating for a little while and he felt like he could trust her with that information. It's clear that even though they've been divorced for a long time, he still has conflicted feelings about the whole situation. Therapy or no therapy."

"It sounds like she was a hypochondriac," Joe mused.

"It sounds like she was desperate for attention," I countered. "Hypochondriac or not. At least hypochondriacs don't use their supposed illness against anybody. He said she would do it before, during and after his business trips."

"She wanted to keep him near her," Darcy mused.

"Which is exactly the sort of thing that pushes somebody away," I pointed out. "I completely understand why he stayed with her as long as he did. I'm sure he still cared for her, and he didn't want to make it look like he was abandoning her when she needed him."

"If all of this is true, he really is a decent guy," Darcy concluded with an unhappy frown. "Why do things have to be complicated? Why couldn't she find a nice, uncomplicated guy?"

"Life is always complicated," Joe replied. I wondered if he was talking more to my sister or to himself. "Nothing is ever cut and dried, no matter how much we want it to be." Lord knew I could agree with that.

"You have cheese on your face." I observed, wiping my cheek with my thumb to indicate where the cheese was on his cheek.

"Did I get it?" he asked after completely missing it. How could he have missed it?

"No. Jeez, Louise. It's right here." I pointed to myself. He swiped his face again, and again the cheese stayed in place. Gosh, you're worse than a child." I reached out and took care of it myself.

And when I glanced at my sister, I found her smirking. I had to bite my tongue to keep from telling her where she could stick that smirk of hers.

I had to change the subject, and fast. "Did Dad tell you I was in to talk to him about Moira's ex-husband and his business partners?"

"That's what you were there for?" he asked, all wide-eyed surprise. "That's funny. I thought you came in to deliver some delicious, homemade baked goods."

"Stop."

"Because you're such a generous person."

"Enough."

"You would never resort to such tactics."

"Do you want more cheese on your face? Because I have extra." I held up what was left of my slice.

He ducked, laughing. "Oh, believe me. He told me all about it."

I decided not to ask why he snickered when he said that. I had the feeling I knew all too well. Dad probably had a lot to say about my visit. Rather than waste precious cheese on his smug face, I asked, "What do you think? Have you looked into these supposedly shady characters Moira might have been doing business with?"

"That really isn't any of your concern."

"Why do you have to do that?"

"Do what?"

"You know exactly what I'm saying. You talk to me the way he talks to me, and I don't like it when he does it. But since he is my father, he gets a pass. You, on the other hand, are not my father. We aren't even related. I don't appreciate you talking down to me."

"I'm not trying to talk down."

"But you are!" I looked to my sister for support. "Right? Isn't he?"

She looked up like she was surprised. "Oh, you remember that I'm here? I was starting to think you forgot about me completely."

"You're no help." I turned back to him, scowling. "Listen, I'm just trying to help. You always talk to me like I'm a nuisance."

"I definitely do not think of you as a nuisance," he

allowed, chuckling. "But you tend to second-guess my work, and I don't appreciate that."

It didn't take long for me to figure out what was going on. "Oh, so he told you that he told me it's insulting for me to stick my nose into things. Right?"

He blinked, shrugging. "I have no idea what you're talking about."

"Tell me another good one," I muttered.

"Listen. And please, take me seriously, because I'm not joking around." He even dropped what was left of his slice on the plate, folding his hands instead. "Bob told us exactly what he told you. He wanted to meet with Moira Banks because the fund he invested in with her husband suddenly stopped paying out, and he hadn't heard anything about the progress into quarters. Right?"

"All right."

"Obviously, if that was the reason they got together, we want to look into it. We contacted the other fund managers and are in the process of acquiring documentation. Believe me, I have no intention of letting this slip through the cracks. If there was anything shady going on, we'll find out. Will also find out who was responsible for that shadiness, and once we do, we'll start asking more pointed questions in their direction. Okay? Is that enough for you?"

I didn't know what bothered me more: how annoyed he sounded, or that my sister witnessed the entire thing. Nobody wanted to be dressed down in public.

Was I stupid, thinking we'd gotten past this point? That he wouldn't take that attitude with me anymore, now that we were friends? There I was, thinking I wasn't the annoying, pesky irritation anymore. Not that we were equals. I wasn't that foolish, I knew he had the training and experience while I was better with a stand mixer and an oven.

I thought we were better than that.

I shrugged it off. "Sure. Fine. Whatever."

"Oh, come on," he sighed. "Don't get angry now."

"I'm not angry," I assured him without so much as a glance, holding up a finger to get the attention of one of the kids behind the counter.

I was angry. Good and angry. Another slice of pizza might not solve anything, but it sure felt like it would just then.

"I think that's my cue to… go and do anything else in the entire world." Darcy slid off her stool, then leaned over to stage whisper to Joe. "And if I were you, I'd find something else to do, too."

"I don't care much either way." I didn't even bother dabbing away the grease this time, folding the slice in half and taking a vicious bite. If Joe took some sort of message from it, good for him.

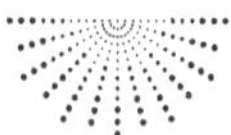

CHAPTER THIRTEEN

"You're sure this is a good idea?"

"You're gonna make me wonder why I called you," I warned Raina.

Her voice bounced around the inside of my car when she laughed. "What? You don't like to hear the truth? That it might've been going a little too far, getting Janice's address and driving to her house?"

"What about it?" I asked as I made the last turn onto Janice's street. This was the neighborhood Bob had lived in with her. The house on the Crest was the home he'd purchased after their divorce. There I was, imagining that beautiful house had belonged to the two of them.

Didn't divorced men normally downsize after the deed was done? Especially when the wife got the house in the divorce?

It was well out past Paradise City, almost an hour up the coast from Cape Hope. This was the last street before the boardwalk and commercial drag which bordered the beach.

"Wow," I whispered. "Can you imagine living virtually up against the ocean?"

"You practically do already," she chuckled.

"Not even. It's like a ten, fifteen-minute walk from my apartment."

"Poor baby."

"Says the girl who grew up in a Manhattan penthouse," I snickered. "Anyway, I do think it's a good idea. I wanna know more about this Bob person. Something tells me his ex-wife won't hold back."

"Remember to be careful. Her side of the story is her side of the story, and if she's bitter…"

"It doesn't sound like she's bitter. A bitter woman would sue for alimony. She didn't."

"That was eight years ago."

"Even so." I pulled up in front of a house that, surprisingly, was somewhat smaller than the one Bob currently owned. But it was no less charming with its corner turret, its bay windows and a picket fence covered in ivy. There were sweet little touches, too. Windchimes, a bird bath, little gnome and frog and fairy statues in the garden.

This was a sweet woman. A whimsical one. Bob had described her as artistic. I decided I liked her already.

"I'll let you know how it goes," I informed my very negative, very unhelpful best friend.

"I wish I was there with you," she confessed before getting off the phone. I couldn't help but feel a little smug as I got out of the car. She could warn me away all she wanted, but she still wished she was with me. That had to say something.

It was a beautiful day, the sort of day that got people out onto the beach. I couldn't see the sand or ocean from where I stood, but there were so many colorful kites hanging in the air. Plenty of people were enjoying themselves out there.

Then, there was me. Sneaking an hour north to harass a woman over her ex-husband.

Was I going too far? Maybe. Even I could admit that. But this was my mom. I wanted to know about the man she may or may not continue dating.

Who may or may not end up on trial for murder. Who Mom couldn't seem to let go of several days after their last meeting at the café. No matter how many times Darcy and I tried to remind her that Bob wasn't the only man in the entire world, she refused to entertain the idea of accepting a date with anyone else.

And she was still getting messages from other interested men, too, since her dating profile was active. No way were we about to let her take it down, especially when it had taken three solid days of edits for Mom to decide it was perfect.

Was he worth all this anguish and effort? I figured I'd go to Janice and find out. No crime in that.

Though my knees knocked a little as I rounded the wraparound porch, hoping Janice didn't see me through a window and call the cops on a supposed intruder. The fact that Joe's voice was still in my head after days of not talking to him—the jerk—and still reminding me that I'd deserve it if the cops showed up because I was, indeed, intruding didn't make me feel much better.

"Hello?" I called out. There was no answer at either the

front or side door, though a car sat in the driveway. Maybe she'd gone for a walk on the beach. I would if I lived mere steps from it.

"Hello?" a female voice called out. "I'm in back!"

She sounded friendly enough. What did I expect? Some withered crone who fired a warning shot before ordering me off her property?

The backyard was like something out of a home and garden magazine. I held my breath in wonder at the lush, fragrant flowers—enormous peonies, hydrangeas, snow white roses, honeysuckle. Bees and butterflies flitted around, and the trickling of water led my gaze to a small pond which held red and orange fish. The soft tinkling of windchimes was music. Further out, tomatoes in all stages of growth from tiny babies to heavy, ruby spheres, trailed up tall stakes.

I sort of wanted to move in, in other words.

In the center of it all sat a woman wearing a wide-brimmed, straw hat and the sort of long, gauzy dress one would expect from a woman whose garden looked like something out of a fantasy. In front of her was an easel and canvas, and she held a pallet in one hand and a paintbrush in the other. She herself might have easily been something out of a painting, right down to her long, silvery hair.

I almost didn't want to disturb her simply because the entire image was too perfect. I wish I could back away and pretend I'd never showed up, but it was a little too late for that.

She turned to me, her face deceptively smooth considering the silver in her hair. She seemed to glow with an inner light. Was this the woman Bob had described? Maybe she didn't live here anymore, maybe the listing I found online was an old one.

"Can I help you?" she asked, and there wasn't so much as a hint of dread or concern at the presence of a total stranger in her garden.

"I'm so sorry to disturb you. Are you Janice Perlman?" I didn't know at that point if I wanted this to be her or not.

"I am." She lowered the palette to her lap, the brush still poised in the air. "Are you here to sell me something? Because I'm not in the mood to buy anything right now."

"Oh, no! No, it's nothing like that." I pressed my palm to my forehead, completely at a loss. What had seemed so important only a few minutes earlier now seemed utterly pointless, a waste of my time. And hers, which made me feel much worse.

It wasn't like I had never wasted my time before. I was actually pretty good at it.

"Are you all right?" she asked, tilting her head to the side as she took in the sight of me unraveling more and more with each passing moment.

"I'm fine, really," I tried to assure her when she looked anything but convinced. "I'm so sorry, I shouldn't have come here and disturbed you. It's just that... Well, I was recently acquainted with your ex-husband, Bob."

She stayed perfectly still except for a slight nod of her head. "All right," she murmured.

"He, ah, knows my mother. And there've been some...

what you might call complications." Holy crap, what was I thinking? I couldn't tell this woman her ex-husband was a suspect in a murder investigation. Bob had already said the two of them weren't really involved in each other's lives, so I doubted she had any reason to know, but I also doubted she would like getting the news from a perfect stranger.

"Complications? Is anything wrong with Bob?" Her brow wrinkled as she frowned.

"Not really." I let out a huge sigh, dropping my hands to my sides. "Really, I just wanted to get an idea of the sort of person he is. I know this is going to sound completely ridiculous, like I'm totally overreacting, but he's the first man my mom has even considered going out with since she divorced my dad years ago. I just want to make sure she's not making any sort of a mistake. He seems like a nice man, but still. She's my mother."

A soft smile tugged at the corners of her mouth. "Why don't you come here and have a seat?" Using her paintbrush, she gestured toward a wicker chair with a thick cushion. "You look a little worn out. Believe me, I know what it's like to feel worn out."

"Thank you, I think I will." The thing was, it wasn't like I was lying. I was concerned for Mom, and I did want to know the sort of person Bob was. Janice didn't need to know anything about Moira's murder.

"You say your mother and Bob have started seeing each other?" she asked as I took a seat in the very comfortable chair.

I nodded. "Recently. It's not that they're serious or anything. I don't know why I feel like I need to explain that."

She chuckled softly. "Trust me, there's been a great deal of water that's passed under the bridge since the divorce. I don't hold any bad feelings toward him at all. He stuck with me much longer than most people would have. I don't know if he told you anything about my health problems."

My eyes went wide. I could only hope I seemed genuinely surprised. "No. He mentioned you and your name, but that was it. He has no idea I'm here, but I guess I don't need to tell you that part."

"Did your mother send you?" Was she teasing? It seemed like she was. There was a little twinkle in her eye and everything.

"Gosh, no!" I laughed. "No, she would be mortified if she knew I'd come. Funny how it's all right for a parent to be overprotective of their child, but not the other way around."

She had a soft, gentle sort of laugh. "Understood. You're just being a good daughter, concerned for your mom. There's nothing wrong with that. You say she hasn't dated in quite some time?"

"Not since the divorce. It's been almost six years now."

"She could do a lot worse than Bob, I'll tell you that. He's a true gentleman, one of the old school sort of men. Faithful to a fault. Like I said, I gave him many opportunities to walk away, and I'm sure most men would have done it long before he did."

I leaned in slightly, curiosity practically overwhelming me. "Why do you say that?"

"As I said, I've had health challenges. They still come and go. The doctors have never been able to diagnose me with anything," she waved a hand, rolling her eyes. "I can't tell you how much of my money they've collected, and for what? Some days I can barely get out of bed. Some days, I don't. They don't think it's autoimmune, they don't think it's anything to do with my nervous system. I'm prone to respiratory infections, migraines, exhaustion. You name it, I've probably had it at one point or another. It's very frustrating, and very draining. To more than just my bank account," she added with a slight groan.

"I'm very sorry," I murmured for lack of anything better to say.

"Thank you. But I don't tell you this to gain sympathy. I just wanted to let you know the sort of man Bob is. He put up with my aches and pains and complaints and migraines and exhaustion for twenty years and more. I never blamed him for finally running out of stamina."

Either she was sincere, or she was the best liar I had ever seen. Then again, even sincerity could have its problems. Nobody wanted to be married to a martyr. She definitely had the saintly act down pat, too.

"So he's generally the sort of man I can trust with somebody so important to me," I concluded with a smile of relief.

"Oh, absolutely," she laughed. "I can provide references signed by a notary that would make you feel better."

"Careful. I might take you up on that."

"There is one fault of his that I think your mother should be aware of, though." Her smile faded, her expression tightening somewhat.

This was it. This was when she was going to tell me he was secretly a monster. Somebody who shouldn't be trusted around women, children or animals.

"He's a complete workaholic." She winced. "I rarely saw him for weeks at a time. He would be gone on business trips, visiting his other stores, board meetings, retreats. Naturally, I wanted to go with him, but my health wouldn't allow for it. And I knew that if I were locked in a hotel room somewhere, he would only worry about me rather than focusing on his work. I didn't want to be a burden."

Yes, she definitely saw herself as a saint. But some people were just like that, especially those who were sick—or, who had convinced themselves they were sick.

I waved a hand, snickering. "That's perfect, then."

"Oh?" Her brows lifted. "How so?"

"My mom's the same way. Total workaholic. She has her own café in Cape Hope, she's been running it for almost my entire life."

"Really? That's interesting. What's it called?"

"Sweet Nothings. She specializes in baked goods. It's right next door to my sister's bookshop, and people come and go between the two places all the time."

"That's a perfect combination! Sounds like the sort of place I'd like to visit. Not just because I would like to get a look at your mother," she added with a playful wink. "I wouldn't tell her who I was." Her smile faded, though. "Of course, I don't drive a lot anymore. I just never know when a migraine's going to hit, and I wouldn't want to be behind the wheel."

"I'm awfully sorry about that," I murmured.

She waved it off, shaking herself a little. "There I go again, sliding into self-pity. And I've been a terrible hostess. I should've offered you something to drink, or a snack."

"No, thank you. Besides, I've already asked enough of you. And I get more than enough snacks at the café, believe me."

She eyed me up and down, chuckling. "Please, you still have that youthful metabolism."

"You sound like my mom," I laughed. "She's always warning me that my metabolism is going to fail me soon."

"A wise woman. And not just because she sees the worth of a good man." She smiled, but it was a fake smile. There was no doubt about it, and I wasn't only telling myself that. I was determined not to see things that didn't exist. She definitely looked troubled all of a sudden.

"I can go," I murmured, suddenly worried that I'd overstayed my welcome. Maybe she was coming down with something, maybe she was suddenly not feeling well. No matter what Bob said, no matter if what was ailing her was only in her head, it was very real to her.

She shook her head. "No, you don't have to. Unless you want to. It's only that something just occurred to me, and I wondered if I should share it with you or not."

If she was trying not to pique my interest, she was failing miserably. Who wouldn't want to know what she was talking about after a lead up like that? "You can tell me. Especially if you think it's something I ought to know, or something my mom should know."

"I don't want you to have the wrong idea. I know how easy it is for an idea to bloom into something completely outlandish. It's only that..."

She looked away from me, toward the pond. "Bob can be

a bit of a jinx. He would kill me if he heard me say that, but it's true."

"Excuse me? Jinx?"

She nodded slowly. "I know, it sounds silly. He always used to tell me how silly it sounded when I would tease him about it. Only, every joke has a grain of truth to it. I wouldn't have simply made up such an accusation, if that's what you want to call it. I wasn't trying to accuse him of anything, though it may have come out that way. I shouldn't have said anything."

I practically jumped at her. "No, please. I won't tell him. It's just between you and me."

"Believe me, he's a good man." She looked at me, and there was a new light in her eyes. She was pleading with me, desperate for me to believe her. "I don't want you to take this as the rambling of a jealous ex-wife. Nothing could be further from the truth. But Bob has this knack for strange things he seems to attract to him. I know, it sounds silly."

"What sort of things are you talking about? I don't understand."

"Little accidents. They don't happen to him, but to the people around him. For instance, he'd just finished fixing one of the stairs inside, leading up to the second floor. The very night after he declared the job done, I fell down the stairs after stepping on that step. It broke, the part of it that hung over the riser simply snapped off. I lost my balance."

Ice landed with a thud in my stomach. He'd talked about her falling downstairs, hadn't he? Though he made it sound like she'd faked it.

Yet here she was, talking about the same thing.

"And then there was the pergola he put together. This was years ago, mind you. He was always handy. I guess you know he works in hardware, or he did before going into semi-retirement. He was very proud of his work. It sat right there." She pointed to where the tomatoes grew. "I wanted to hang a sheet underneath to protect the tomatoes from the sun. Only one of the beams fell on my head."

I gasped. "Oh my gosh! Was it heavy?"

"Well, it was a two-by-four. I didn't exactly take the time to weigh it. It was very solid." She grimaced, staring at that area of the garden. "I had a concussion, and an absolutely blinding headache for almost an entire week. It took ages for the bump to heal. I understand that's the way of it with head injuries."

I shuddered.

She then turned to me. "I know through mutual friends that the first woman he dated after the divorce was in a car accident when her brakes failed. She'd only just had the car serviced not even a week earlier, and even after an investigation, no one could figure out what happened. She made it out all right, she managed to pull over to the side of the road before crashing into anything or anybody. It might've been much, much worse. Now, I don't think Bob had anything to do with that, any more than he had anything to do with my accidents. But you can see where a person would start to wonder if he isn't jinxed."

Jinxed? It sounded like a lot more than that to me. "What was the name of that friend?" I asked.

"Sarah Jackson. She lives here, in town." She gave me directions; it was close enough to walk. "I mean, not that you need to see her but, you might get an idea of the sort of person he is from her, as well. If you're still interested."

Interested? Nothing could have kept me away.

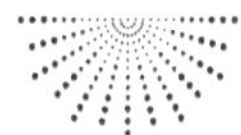

CHAPTER FOURTEEN

"My accident? Gosh, that was years ago! Who told you about that?"

Sarah Jackson sat with me on her front porch. I could understand why she didn't want to invite me in, being a stranger and everything. Part of me would've loved the chance to take a look inside. I'd seen enough rambling Victorians in Cape Hope to know how exquisite they could be inside, and this place reminded me a lot of them.

"Janice Perlman. I was just visiting with her. You see, I only wanted to know more about Bob since he and my mom are friends and, you know. Maybe I'm a little overprotective. She's been out of the game for a long time."

Guilt practically choked me. She would kill me if she knew I was airing her laundry all over town—the very same thing I usually got furious with her over. I was being such a hypocrite, though I told myself again and again it was all for her benefit.

Which was probably exactly the same sort of thing she

told herself about me. Like mother, like daughter. If I started wearing splashy floral prints, I'd be in big trouble.

"Oh, Bob." She smiled a little, leaning back in her rocking chair. She had the whole wealthy retiree look going on, right down to the sweater knotted around her shoulders. Did people actually dress that way when they were just sitting around the house? It wasn't like we were out shopping or at the golf course or some other fancy place. Like a champagne brunch or something. "Bob was a lot of fun. He's a nice man. Not for me, not long-term, but nice."

"And why is that? If you don't mind my asking, of course."

She waved it off. "Maybe he was too nice for me. I think that's always been my problem. That's the reason my husband is my ex-husband. It's why I haven't managed to hold onto a man for longer than a few months at a time since my divorce. When a man is too nice to me, I decide he has ulterior motives and I push him away." She spoke like a woman who'd been talking to a therapist for a while. Clearly, it wasn't doing any good, if she was still repeating the same old patterns.

"Well, I guess of all the reasons to break things off with him, that's hardly a bad one," I offered.

"I just can't believe Janice brought up that accident. Gosh, it was so silly. Granted, I was shaken up for days afterward, to the point where I didn't want to get behind the wheel. But I got over it. What?" She leaned in a little, frowning. "Did she suggest Bob had something to do with that?"

"Not directly," I was quick to assure her. "Maybe indirectly. I don't know, she called him a jinx, and your accident was one of the examples she gave."

"A jinx? That's rich, coming even from her," she laughed. "I mean, you never know what's going to come out of her mouth, but that's a new one."

"You mean to say she's unreliable?"

"No, I wouldn't go that far." She touched her hand to her perfectly groomed bob, a rich chestnut color which I suspected wasn't quite natural for a woman her age. She was easily older than Mom, with the sort of lined face that spoke of a life spent outdoors.

Maybe that was why Mom had aged so well. She was always inside, out of the sun, though she was still active and on her feet throughout the day.

Sarah sighed. "Janice is a free spirit, I guess you could say. She's a little too young to have been a hippie, but that's what they would've called her if she was born ten or fifteen years earlier. She's the sort of person who would think of a jinx. I always thought she was a little bit flighty. And more than a little obsessed with her supposed health issues. She doesn't look unhealthy, does she?"

"Not all illnesses are visible on the outside," I reminded her in a soft voice. Why I felt the need to defend this perfect stranger was beyond me, but it didn't seem fair for Sarah to talk about her that way.

"Of course, it was very petty of me to say that. But that doesn't change what's behind what I said. A lot of what she says and believes needs to be taken with a grain of salt. Accidents are accidents."

Sure, but I knew something neither of these women did.

This man who seemed to attract accidents like honey attracted flies just so happened to be in the presence of a certain woman hours before she was most likely murdered. Knowing what I knew, it wasn't so easy to laugh off Janice's concerns as nothing more than the ramblings of an eccentric woman.

"Your accident," I prompted, since we were going off track by gossiping about Janice. "Is it true your car was only just serviced not long before that?"

"Yes, and no one could say for sure exactly what happened. I mean, what are the odds of brake lines suddenly snapping?"

Wait.

"What did you say?" I whispered. "Your brake lines were cut?"

Her mouth fell open like she'd never heard this or even thought of it, though it was the first thing that came to my mind. "Cut? Of course not. Who would cut my brake lines?"

"I think you would know better than I would." Was this woman insane? Or was she determined not to see the truth of what happened to her, even years later?

She shrugged, clearly not caring. "All I know is, my car was working just fine while I drove to meet with Bob for dinner. Yet on the way back, I couldn't stop the darn thing. I know I'm lucky I pulled off the road in time. Since my car was visible from where we ate dinner, I think it's safe to say no one managed to pop the hood and cut the lines while I sat not twenty feet away."

It was unlikely, but not impossible.

"Do you mind my asking how close you and Bob

Perlman were?" I ventured. "I don't need the specifics, of course, but in general?"

"We didn't date for long," she sighed. "As I said, he was too nice for me. We saw each other on and off for a few months before deciding it wasn't going anywhere."

"I see," I murmured. That wasn't true. I didn't see anything. And the more I learned, the deeper my confusion grew. "By any chance, would you know of anyone else who Bob dated? Mutual friends, that sort of thing?"

"I think he was casually involved with a couple of acquaintances we share," she allowed, giving me their names. "I don't mean to paint the picture of a player. Isn't that what they're called nowadays?"

"Something like that," I murmured, trying to smile. "And believe me, I'm not here to judge anyone. I mean, yeah, I would like to know more about him for my mom's sake. But I don't think dating several women over the course of eight years is anything worth being concerned over."

I left her not long after that, since my brain was moving a hundred miles a minute and my conversation skills had taken a nosedive thanks to so many new questions.

Rather than getting in the car and zipping my way back down the parkway, I took notes on my phone while everything was still fresh in my mind. I found that doing a brain dump like that, so to speak, helped me later on. It would make it easier to get everything organized and plan the next steps.

Were Janice's accidents really accidents? If they weren't, who caused them? Was she a hypochondriac, desperate for attention, the way Bob described her?

Or was he as callous as he was afraid Mom would think he was? Maybe it was guilt making him assume she would see him that way.

What about Sarah? Would Bob have had time to cut her brake lines while they were at the restaurant? Even if she excused herself, he would've had to go outside, somehow pop the hood, cut the lines, and hurry back into the restaurant in time for her to not know anything had gone on. Or did she have enemies elsewhere?

What about these other women? I would have to go to the library, maybe, and do a little digging. Had they been in accidents like Sarah's close call?

What would Bob have to gain from causing these issues? It was one thing for a husband to plot his wife's death, especially when she was independently wealthy. Money was, after all, the root of so many evils. But what would he have to gain from hurting or even killing Sarah, or the other women? And what would he have had to gain by killing Moira?

Motive was something that hadn't really been discussed yet, at least not in front of me. Mostly, I guessed, because there was no easy motive to be pinpointed. If he'd done it, it would more likely have been a crime of passion. One of those in-the-moment sort of things, something done in the heat of the moment that couldn't be taken back once a person was in their right mind again.

The sort of thing that happened to Sarah, on the other hand, wasn't in the heat of the moment. It would've taken thought and planning.

By the time I finished taking my notes, I was no closer to

having things figured out than I'd been when I got in the car. But it was a start. I knew that once I had a little time to research and maybe ask more questions, I would have a clearer picture of who Bob Perlman really was.

"And then we'll see who really knows what they're talking about," I whispered with a vindictive smile as I started the car and pulled away from the curb.

Joe Sullivan would regret being so snippy with me once he saw he wasn't the only one who could conduct an investigation.

CHAPTER FIFTEEN

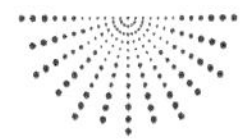

"Mom?" I called out, flinging the front door open. "Mom, where are you?"

In my other hand, the one I hadn't used to practically break down the front door, I held my phone. On the screen was the message Trixie had sent. *Emergency, get to your mom's as soon as you can.*

One couldn't possibly estimate how many awful scenarios had run through my head on seeing that. What on earth could have happened? Had she experienced a suspicious accident of her own? I imagined her lying at the bottom of the stairs, electrocuted in the bathtub.

When she came strolling out of the kitchen, wiping her hands on a dish towel, I was both immensely relieved and maybe slightly irritated.

"Emma? What on earth is the matter? You look like you saw a ghost after getting picked up and tossed around by a tornado." Truly, nobody could put me down while expressing concern like Sylvia Harmon.

I dropped onto the sofa, my muscles sagging with relief. "You're okay?" I managed to ask while trying to catch my breath. For sure, nothing looked out of place.

"Oh, good. You're here!" Trixie followed Mom out of the kitchen and clapped her hands on finding me sitting there. What was left of me, anyway.

"What the heck? What were you thinking, sending me a message like that?" I didn't often let any minor irritation show in my voice, not when it came to her. I knew she meant well, and her long friendship with Mom left me wanting to avoid coming between them in any way.

But just then, I was ready to smack her silly for scaring me.

"You are such a worrywart." She laughed, which definitely had the opposite of what I guessed her intended effect was. Instead of calming me, she managed to infuriate me more.

"Usually, when someone says there's an emergency and I need to come to Mom's house right away—let's not forget how low she's been feeling lately—I tend to jump to a negative conclusion. Call me crazy, but that's just how I roll." I crossed my arms over my chest, blowing out an exasperated sigh.

Mom turned to Trixie, shaking her head. "Why would you scare her that way? Honest-to-goodness, sometimes I'm convinced you don't think at all about the consequences of the things you do." Coming from Mom, that was quite a reprimand. She was almost always patient and generous to a fault when it came to the people she cared about.

"I'm sorry. But I felt this was an emergency situation." Trixie seemed completely unaffected by Mom's frustration.

"What's going on in here?" I should've known Nell had something to do with this, too. She came out of the kitchen carrying a pitcher. "Who's up for sangria?"

I had walked into some sort of bizarro-world. That could be the only explanation. "You mean to tell me the big emergency I had to come here for was nothing more than you wanting me to come by for sangria?"

Trixie held up both hands. "Okay, okay. Let's all control ourselves. Let's not allow our tempers to get out of hand. I admit, I could have given a little more thought to the words I used."

"For heaven's sake, you're a journalist. I would think you'd know better." Sangria or not, I wasn't about to let her off the hook that easily. "You know how worried I've been about her lately."

"Please, don't talk about me as if I were Lola," Mom chided. "I am standing right here."

"You know what I mean," I sighed. "I've been worried. That's not a secret."

"We've all been concerned," Nell agreed. "Which is why we're here now. To help lift your mother's spirits."

"And since you and your detective friend are fighting…" Trixie began with an arch expression.

I cut her off, glaring at my mother. "Seriously?"

"Well, you are fighting."

"We're really not. I'm irritated with him and I haven't spoken to him since a few nights ago. I guess Darcy couldn't wait to tell you all about it."

"Emma Jane, you are pouting." Mom wagged a finger at me, then waved me into the kitchen. "Come on. I have brownies in the oven. I thought some dark chocolate might go with our wine."

I wanted to stay strong. I wanted to pout and be annoyed and hold onto my righteous indignation, as if that would punish Trixie for getting me so worked up.

But who was I kidding? Brownies were brownies, especially the dark chocolate kind. People who didn't like dark chocolate didn't know what they were talking about. This was coming from me, the Queen of all things sugary.

I still made sure everybody knew I was only accepting a glass of wine begrudgingly, because I was very mature like that. "So what is this? An intervention for the two of us?" I asked, settling in on a stool at the counter. It was the best place to be if I wanted first dibs on the brownies in the oven.

"Not an intervention," Trixie chuckled, leaning against the counter with her own glass in hand. "More like a girls night." Just my luck, getting pulled into a girls night with three women much older than me with whom I had no desire to discuss my personal life.

That sangria certainly went down smooth. I would need quite a bit of it I was going to get through this.

"Sometimes I wonder if men are worth it at all," Nell mused, sipping her wine with a sigh.

"What is it? Trouble in paradise with Rance?" I asked. I hadn't heard anything about this, probably because everyone was so busy being focused on Mom and Bob at the moment.

With a glance at Mom, she shook her head. She looked regretful, like she wished she could commiserate more, given the situation. I had never known anyone to look like they regretted their relationship going well. "No, not exactly. Still, even when he doesn't intend to annoy me, he reminds me of why it was so easy to spend so many years without a man in my life."

"Men have their uses." Trixie snickered, winking at me when I rolled my eyes. "What? They do. You're a grown up. Don't tell me you don't know what I mean."

"Trixie, my mother is right here." Besides, it wasn't like I was in the mood to talk that way with my elders. No wonder she'd used the word emergency. She probably knew that if she'd called this what it was, I wouldn't have shown up.

I definitely would have come up with an excuse. A burst appendix, maybe. I'd burst it myself if that was what it came to.

"Oh, grow up."

I had the feeling Trixie had already been sampling the wine for a while before I showed up. Maybe that was another reason why she'd been a little extreme with her verbiage via text.

"Are you going to tell me to grow up, too?" Mom asked. "I'm not one of these mothers who treats her daughters like they're her best friends."

"Ouch," I murmured, taking another sip.

"You know what I mean." She sighed. "Certain things do not need to be discussed, girls night or no."

"What's going on with Joe?" Nell asked, patting me on the shoulder. "What did you two fight over?"

I was going to need a lot more wine if this was the way conversation was going to trend. Maybe an entire pitcher just for me. "It's nothing serious. Friends argue all the time. I didn't like the attitude he took with me, and he didn't bother trying to apologize for hurting my feelings, so he can pound sand. There's a beach about a mile down the road, he's more than welcome to get started anytime he wants to."

"Men are swine." Trixie gulped down the last of her glass before holding it out for more.

"You just got finished saying they had their uses," I reminded her.

"Outside of that, they're swine. Why do you think I've stayed single all this time? Casual dating is one thing, but commitment? Please."

"Commitment isn't all that bad," Mom murmured, swirling her wine and sounding thoughtful. "I quite enjoyed it when it was my turn."

I shot Trixie a dirty look, and to her credit, she managed to appear regretful. "Don't pay attention to her," I teased. "She's had a little too much to drink."

"Have not," Trixie insisted.

"Congratulations. You managed to slur words without s's in them." I ducked the playful smack she tried to deliver.

"Don't let Trixie's gloomy attitude change your mind," Nell urged Mom, rubbing her shoulder. "And don't let this little problem with Bob turn you off dating altogether. There's nothing wrong with wanting to be with somebody, to share your life with someone. And you've built such a nice life. You have every right to want to share that with another person."

Now this, I could get behind. Nell usually was the one who spoke sense. "She's right. Just because things aren't working out with Bob doesn't mean they won't work at all. He's not the only man in the world, Mom. Don't get hung up on him like this."

"You don't know how it is," she sighed. "You just don't know."

"Mom. Look at me." I took her hand, resting on the countertop. "You know very well that I was counting on a proposal from Landon. I thought that was what I wanted more than anything else in the world. I was so sure he was the one. I was practically planning the wedding in my head already. And look what happened. It just goes to show you, just because you think somebody is right doesn't mean they are."

My words of wisdom didn't exactly have their desired effect. "You think I don't know that? The woman who was divorced from her husband of twenty years? You don't think I'm well aware of how many ways there are for things to go south? That's all I've been thinking of since the divorce was finalized. That's what's been keeping me alone, on my own, without any sort of romantic relationship or even casual fling since then. Because you're right. Sometimes, there's just no way of knowing. What we think and what is true aren't necessarily the same thing. Sometimes they're not even close."

I held out my glass, which Nell filled, probably a little too generously. It was going to be a long night.

"You know what she means, though," Trixie piped up, coming to my rescue. "Sure, Bob seems like a real catch. But here you are, starting out your relationship pointing out that he was keeping things from you. Sure, he had his reasons, but still."

"It couldn't hurt to broaden your horizons a bit and answer some of these other men who are sending you messages," Nell ventured. That meant a lot coming from her, being the ever-present voice of reason in Mom's life. Trixie was the troublemaker.

The fact that I was a troublemaker in Raina's life didn't escape me for one second. Was it true that people were only the sum total of the people they knew? If so, I could pretty much break down the different aspects of my personality and attribute them to the people I'd grown up around.

"I can't do that," Mom argued. "Not because I'm in love with Bob or anything like that. I can't just shut my feelings on and off. I wish I could. And honestly, I don't know if the effort is worth it. Why put myself through all the trouble if there's a chance of only getting hurt again?"

The beeping of the oven couldn't have come at a better time. I practically jumped off my stool and grabbed the nearest potholder. "I'll get it," I announced, though I was sure I didn't need to announce anything.

"Then just have fun!" Trixie urged her. "Get out there, let yourself be adored by a man or two. You don't have to exchange vows, for heaven's sake."

"She does have a point," I admitted while pulling the pan from the oven. "You're a total catch. Gorgeous and worthy of adoration."

"Are you talking to me or to the brownies?" Mom teased. The fact that she could tease at all seemed like a good sign.

"The brownies," I retorted, sticking out my tongue. "But it applies to you, too."

She threw back her head with a sigh, staring up at the ceiling. "Maybe you're right. Maybe I did let myself get too wrapped up, too quickly. He's a very nice man, and I love spending time with, but he also seems conflicted over his past and it's very complicated. Maybe I don't need that sort of complication in my life."

"There you go! That's what I want to hear." Trixie raised her glass—a little unsteadily, I noticed—and toasted my mother. "To moving on," she announced.

"Now, we just have to get your love life sorted out," Nell announced, slinging an arm over my shoulders.

"Can I have some more?" I asked, thrusting my glass toward her.

CHAPTER SIXTEEN

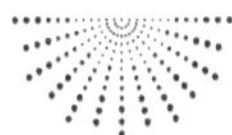

The morning after our little girls night was very much like the morning after most ill-advised girls nights. I walked through my apartment as slowly as possible, my feet barely touching the floor. Even the sound of them hitting the wood while I wasn't wearing shoes made me wince.

"Don't look at me that way," I warned Lola when she stared at me, looking disappointed. "I don't get all judgy toward you when you make bad decisions. Besides, I wasn't the one who fixed up the sangria. That stuff is evil. If anybody ever offers you any, you tell them to take it somewhere else. Understood?"

I decided that a lick on the back of my hand was her way of agreeing. It was probably the only part of my body that didn't hurt.

"Meanwhile," I continued, "I seem to remember telling Nell that we needed to slow down a little with mixing up pitcher after pitcher, and she didn't listen. So don't judge me."

Even in my utter agony, I had to laugh at myself. "There I go again, forgetting you aren't human."

And there she went again, giving me one of her looks. "Don't blame me," I muttered. "It's not my fault you're only a dog."

Talking to the dog was a nice way to distract myself from the shape I was in, but that couldn't last forever. I had to get on with my day, one painful step at a time. A handful of ibuprofen and a ton of water helped a lot, to the point where I could actually stand the thought of making myself a greasy breakfast sandwich.

Everybody knew greasy food was the best cure after a night of too much sangria.

A bacon, egg and cheese was just what the doctor ordered. After that, and a shower, I loaded Lola into her little stroller and set off for the library. Why had I told Nell I would see her there? That was the mystery I hoped to solve upon arrival.

And solve it, I did. But not before my auntie stared at me with a look of utter disgust. "I honestly didn't think we drank that much at the time," she whispered when I met her at the desk. It was almost noon, but she still looked a little green.

"Tell me about it." I would've shaken my head, only it might've fallen off if I did. Things were still a little touch and go. "That's what girls night will get you."

"At least your mother seemed to be in better spirits by the time we left," she whispered.

"True, and she didn't have that much to drink." Clearly, she was the most mature and responsible of all of us, keeping in mind the fact that the café would need to be opened bright and early. She'd given me the day off, so to speak—technically, since I didn't get paid, I wasn't exactly an employee.

"So, you're here to do your research?" she asked.

"That's a good question. Here's the thing, I don't remember telling you that I had research to do." I winced, embarrassed. It wasn't like me to forget.

Besides, I had to wonder what else I might've said that slipped my memory. Something less innocent than having research to do.

Nell shook her head slightly, then stopped with a look of pain. I wasn't the only one afraid my head would fall off if I wasn't careful. "Holy cow, you did enjoy more than a few glasses, didn't you?"

"It all gets fuzzy after my third brownie," I admitted. "That's around the time you guys started talking about the boyfriends you had back in high school, and I guess I wanted to numb myself out of the discomfort."

"Sorry about that," she sighed. "We were just trying to get her mind off of things."

I completely understood, of course, though I might have been scarred for life. This entire situation from beginning to end had been quite eye-opening. I was seeing parts of my mother that I had never imagined, nor that I really needed to know about.

There was a difference between knowing my mother was still a woman and actually having it proven out loud.

"So you don't remember pulling me aside and confessing you visited a certain someone's ex-wife yesterday?" She fixed me with a knowing look as I groaned, remembering. "What were you thinking?"

"If I had the brainpower available to me right now, I might be able to tell you." I sighed. "I just wanted to get a better idea of him. And I think I did. In fact, I think I learned more than I wanted to learn."

Funny how that snapped her out of her misery. Her eyes were bright again. "What do you mean?"

"I will tell you this, but you have to swear you won't say a word to anybody else. Not even Trixie. Especially not Trixie, because you know she'll end up saying something to Mom."

"Is it that serious?"

"It might be. I'm not sure yet. Promise?"

She looked offended. "You know I do."

Yes, I knew she did, and that would have to be enough. I gave her the basic rundown of what I'd learned, and of the fact that I also learned the names of another two potential victims. "Now, we don't know anything definite, so let's not jump to conclusions."

What a silly thing to say, since Trixie had already jumped. The woman was practically freefalling into a pit of speculation. "That pig," she snarled. "Who does he think he is? He has another think coming if he thinks we'll let him get away with something like that with Sylvia."

"Again," I urged, "don't jump to conclusions. We don't know the real situation yet. But I wanted to look into these other women and see if there was ever anything in the papers about them having an accident or something strange happening to them, I don't know. I'm flailing around in the dark here."

"By all means, look away. Don't forget to tell me what you found." Only then did she look over the desk and notice Lola staring up at her, expectant. "Forgive me, Lola. I didn't say hello to you first."

"She's in a snippy mood today," I decided, reaching over to pet her.

"How can you tell?"

"The present she left in my shoes this morning was one indicator." I scowled at the dog, who at least had the decency to hide her face in her paws.

With that, I wheeled the stroller over to the computers. Part of me wondered if I could convince Nell to give me a password to get into the periodical database from my laptop rather than having to come down to the library every time I wanted to look at old newspapers, but that would rob me of the chance to say hi to her.

Not to mention the fact that I had always loved the library, and not just because she worked there. The nerd in me—and that was a very, very large part of me—loved being in the library. Around so many books, so many ideas.

"Hence the reason why I didn't date much in high school," I whispered as I took a seat with Lola securely beside me.

The two names which Sarah had provided were still in my phone. Bonnie Wyatt and Laura Francis. I had looked them both up online from home, but of course, there wasn't much to be found. Neither of them had a social media presence. No big surprise there, since there were still people of their generation who didn't see the value of social media.

Sometimes, I found myself agreeing with them. Even though social media had helped me build my brand and gotten me my job with Haute Cuisine, it could also be the bane of my existence.

"How should I go about this?" I asked my dog, who obviously had nothing to say about the matter. "Why am I even talking to you? You're the one who pooped in my shoe today. You little stinker—literally."

I turned my attention back to the computer and the database waiting for me to plug in a search term. I typed in Bonnie's name and on a whim added the word *accident*. Clearly, I would come up with nothing, since all of this was a guessing game and I had absolutely no idea why I was even wasting my time this way.

Which was why I just about jumped out of my chair when I got a hit.

I leaned in, whispering to myself as I read.

In what could only be described as a freak accident, the hairdryer under which Mrs. Wyatt sat at the salon on Atlantic Avenue suddenly sparked and caught fire. Fortunately, Mrs. Wyatt was able to escape from the device before her hair was set ablaze, but the ensuing flames caused enough damage to the salon's equipment that the business will be closed for the foreseeable future while the owner sees to repairs.

What the heck? The poor woman's hairdryer had suddenly caught fire? What in the world? The article was more than five years old. I wondered whether this was around the time she and Bob were dating and wished I'd thought to ask Sarah if she knew any more specifics.

This left me less concerned about Bob being the culprit. Of course, a man would stick out like a sore thumb in a beauty salon. Either another woman had done it, which I couldn't imagine, or it really was nothing more than an accident.

Though wouldn't it be funny if Bob had been dating Bonnie at the time? Maybe Janice was right. Maybe he was a jinx. And maybe Mom was dodging a bullet by not spending more time with him.

I had to look up Elise and see if anything had happened to her. "Son of a gun," I whispered, smiling in a mixture of triumph and disbelief as yet another article appeared. This one involved car trouble again. And again, it could've ended terribly.

"What did you find?"

I jumped a mile, then whirled around to find Nell standing behind me. "Don't do that!" I hissed.

"Sorry. Did you find anything?"

I waved her over and pointed to the screen, where she read what I just had. It seemed Elise had nearly been pinned between her car and her garage. The only reason the story had made the news was the lawsuit she'd threatened against the manufacturer, claiming there had to be some sort of failure in the car's system that allowed it to roll backward down her driveway and almost kill her.

"And the other woman was almost fried under a hairdryer," I added when Nell gasped after finishing the article. "Both of these women were almost injured or worse in freak accidents. I don't know if this was when they were dating Bob but come on. Doesn't that seem a little strange?"

"It doesn't mean he had anything to do with it," she whispered.

"Of course not. And I think we can assume the one in the salon was definitely not him. Who knows? Maybe there's something to be said for a person being jinxed. Maybe he's just bad luck. I mean, things like that have to happen, don't they? Or else, where would people come up with the idea that such things existed in the first place?"

"Everything has to start somewhere," she murmured.

"Exactly. I mean, if it's as simple as this, I feel a little better—though I'm still glad he's not around Mom right now, since she doesn't need the oven to explode out of nowhere."

"Don't even hint at something like that," she whispered, throwing a dirty look my way.

"See? You're superstitious, too. You do believe things like that are possible."

"I simply don't believe in putting a thought like that out into the world. You never know what might come back. If that's superstition, so be it."

"Except for Moira, it wasn't just a freak accident." It was so easy to lose sight of her in the middle of so many other things. When Mom was my priority, I tended to forget about the woman whose murder had set things in motion.

Sitting back with a sigh, I whispered, "This is easily the most complicated situation I've ever been part of. Even more so than the mess at the convention." And that was saying something. Nell knew just as well as I did what an absolute mess that weekend had been, with hundreds and hundreds of writers and professionals gathered at a single resort where someone had been killed. There'd been an endless list of potential killers, with people coming and going all the time and making things more complicated by the second.

This particular case had something that one didn't. This one involved my mother, if only indirectly.

My phone buzzed with a text as Nell went back to her work, and I was glad she had, since the message happened to be from somebody we'd only just been talking about last night. I was both irritated and relieved to see Joe's message. *Where have you been? Free for lunch? Wanted to catch you up on what's happening.*

My thumbs could barely move fast enough. Maybe that was a good thing, since it slowed me down and kept me from saying what I really wanted to say. I went with: *Oh? I deserve a rundown of what's going on? To what do I owe this honor?*

Don't be that way, he replied.

"Don't be that way," I muttered to myself as I got my things together. Easy for him to say. He wasn't the one who'd been humiliated.

That didn't mean I wouldn't be meeting him for lunch, though. Who was I to pass up the opportunity to learn more about the investigation?

"But he's paying," I assured my dog as I rolled her out of the library. "And I might pick the most expensive thing on the menu."

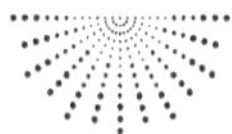

CHAPTER SEVENTEEN

"Ever tried the lobster in this place?"

I was convinced Joe's eyes were a millisecond away from falling out of his head.

"Excuse me?" he asked, barely holding back a laugh.

"Well, you said you were paying. I thought I would be adventurous."

"You told me I was paying," he reminded me with a sour expression. "And I think adventurous is the right word for diner lobster, if you get what I'm saying. Unless you feel like having a close, intimate relationship with your toilet for the next couple of days, you might wanna avoid it."

"You're just a snob," I muttered, looking over the menu again. Obviously, I wasn't about to order the lobster. Though I could if I felt like it.

"I happen to enjoy not getting food poisoning," he whispered.

"Then why are we eating here if you think I could get food poisoning?"

"Why are you being such a baby?"

"This is your way of trying to make things up with me? Because you're doing a really great job." I snapped the menu shut, glaring at him from across the table. "Why in the world would you ask me to come to lunch if all you're going to do is insult me the entire time?"

"Why did you agree to come, if you were going to act this way?"

I rolled my eyes and wished he wasn't right. But he was absolutely right, and we both knew it. "Okay. Fine. I'll play nice. You deserve it after reaching out. And for generously accepting the fact that you will, indeed, be paying for this meal."

"It's the least I can do. I was harsh the other night, I admit it."

I decided to take that as a victory, and to refrain from rubbing it in his face. "Apology accepted."

"So. How've you been?"

"Honestly? I started off today with a hangover."

He winced. "The culprit?"

"My mother, Trixie, Nell, and a few pitchers of sangria."

He winced, teeth bared. "That's a dangerous combination if ever I heard one."

"Tell me about it. My poor liver is still curled up in a corner of my body, trembling and crying and wondering what it did to deserve what I put it through."

"Let me guess. It started out as a way to pick up your mom's spirits."

Sure, let him believe it was entirely about that. Let him

continue being blissfully unaware of his indirect involvement. "Pretty much."

"Did it at least work?"

"I think so. Though I can't say a hangover is worth it."

"You should get a burger or something like that. Something greasy."

"I already covered that at breakfast time. Though I might still follow your advice." Besides, since when was I the girl who refused a greasy meal? I really did need to get my habits under control.

"I thought I would let you know we've been interviewing a lot of people." He placed his menu on the table, pushing it aside in favor of facing me head-on.

I hated how much I had missed his dumb face.

This was exactly what I didn't want to happen. I didn't want to come to rely on him, to become accustomed to his face like they said in that old song from that old musical. It was exactly what I was afraid would happen when he'd announced transferring to Cape Hope.

Against my better judgment, he had become part of my life.

"Have you learned anything?" I asked. Was I playing it cool? I was playing it cool. I hoped.

"Not much more than we already knew," he admitted with a sigh. He sat back against the padded booth, loosening his tie. "I don't think Moira Banks had a real, genuine friend to her name. On one hand, I feel sorry for her. On the other hand, I have to wonder what was wrong with her that she couldn't attract and maintain friends."

"What sort of feeling did you get from these women you've been talking to?"

"They're all pretty catty, petty. I don't think I'd want to be friends with them, either."

"I bet some of them wanted to be friends with you." I winked.

"Do you two know what you want?" our server asked. I hadn't realized she already reached the table, and my cheeks went pink knowing she heard what I said. It wasn't half as bad as some of the things we'd been caught saying in diners and restaurants, but I was still embarrassed.

Joe was diplomatic enough to hold back his laughter until we were on our own again. "Your sense of timing is impeccable."

"Shut up. And tell me I'm wrong. Tell me none of them flirted with you."

"I would. I wish I could. But I can't, because it would be a lie." He scrubbed a hand over the top of his head, smiling ruefully. "I feel like I need to shower."

"The perils of being a handsome detective." I folded my hands under my chin and batted my eyelashes.

"You think I'm handsome?" he teased.

"Shut. Up. We've already had this discussion, you vain thing."

"Oh, right. We have. Anyway, your guess is as good as mine when it comes to who might've had it out for her. We're still looking into that fund Bob was involved in, and I can imagine how frustrated he must've been at their unwillingness to be transparent. Here I am with a badge and an order from a judge, and they're still dragging their feet. He must've been ready to—" He stopped himself before he finished that thought.

Naturally, I finished it for him. "Strangle somebody?" I asked with a smirk.

He didn't smile. "I was going to say kill someone, but close enough. It seems like everybody's determined to stand in the way of this case being solved. Frankly, I don't know that anybody cares how or why she died. It's enough to really make a person think."

"Yeah, that's very sad. Make me a promise?"

"Within reason." he half-smiled. "I know better than to say yes without setting any sort of rules in place."

"I was only going to ask that if I ever get murdered, you would at least want to know who did it."

"At the rate we go, I'll be the one to do it."

"Wow, I sure am glad I'm spending time with you right now."

The thing was, that was true. Sometimes the truth could be wrapped up in a joke, but that didn't make it any less true. I was glad to be with him, very glad. As much as we joked around and pretended to argue, I liked when we were together. It was preferable to not seeing each other at all.

"I promise you. When you finally push somebody too far and they decide to rid the world of your presence, I will definitely see to it the culprit is caught."

"I like how you used the word when, and not if."

"I'm a realist," he shrugged.

He was lucky the food came when it did. "Can I get some ranch dressing?" I asked. "Sorry, I forgot to ask for it before." Probably because I was embarrassed.

"What do you have against ketchup?" Joe asked.

I looked up from taking the lettuce and tomato off the bun. Who wanted soggy, limp, warm lettuce? "I don't have anything against ketchup."

"It has sugar in it. I would think that alone would make you a fan."

"Boy, you've been saving up your best snarky insults over the last few days, haven't you? Is there a little notebook somewhere, where you write these things down and save them for later?"

"Who told you about my notebook?" When he finally stopped laughing at himself, he asked, "So what have you been doing? Keeping yourself busy, I bet?"

"Now that you mention it, yes. I've been keeping myself very busy. Promise you won't get mad."

"Oh, boy. I love the way this is starting out."

"I didn't do anything wrong."

"Yet you think I'll get mad," he observed, shoving a few fries in his mouth and chewing very hard. Much harder than french fries required.

"I may or may not have paid a visit to Bob's ex-wife." I winced, holding up my knife and fork like they would do anything to defend me.

"You did what?" he whispered.

"I, um, visited Janice Perlman. Listen," I continued even though he scowled. "I didn't say anything about the investigation or about Moira, not at all. Everything I talked about had to do with him, in relation to my mom. I told her I just wanted to know more about him because I was concerned for Mom, since she hadn't dated in years and he was her first semi-serious attempt at getting back out there. That's all."

He was very quiet. Too quiet.

Finally, I had to ask, "Are you okay?" The way his chest kept rising and falling was making me nervous.

"I'm trying to breathe. I am focused on my breathing, so stress and anxiety will not get the better of me."

He might as well have started speaking Greek. "Oh. Well, that's good. I'm glad you learned something from the yoga class we went to."

"Actually, I've been attending on my own. While you were out of town, I got into it. We never got the chance to talk about it. I completely forgot to tell you."

"Well, that's great. I'm really glad for you."

"You should be, since it's helping me right now. I'm fighting against the urge to strangle you. So far, it's working."

"For heaven's sake."

He thrust a fry my way. "No, you don't get to take an attitude with me right now. You have no business going out there and bothering that woman."

"I didn't bother anybody!"

"You sure about that? It would bother the hell outta me, having you show up and grill me on my personal life."

"She was very nice. Besides, she turned me onto another possible angle to the case. Granted, I don't think anything will come of it."

"No, I know nothing will come of it."

"Would you stop for just once? Jeez, Louise. You're not my father, though it seems like the more time you spend around him, the more confused you get about that. I don't have to listen to you. I can do what I want."

"If you're obstructing this investigation in any way—"

"No way! It just so happens that a few of the women Bob dated met with strange accidents. His wife did, too, while they were together."

Bingo. That took him by surprise.

"What?" I asked with a sweet smile. "Did you not know about that, Detective?"

"What kind of accidents?" he asked, suspicious. His right eyebrow always twitched when he got suspicious—and the fact that I knew that told me I'd made him feel suspicious more than a few times.

I gave him the rundown, since nothing would come of me torturing him and teasing him and reminding him that I had been one to discover this, not him. "Who knows? Maybe I should be the one to talk to Moira's so-called friends. Women tend to share more with each other than they do with men, even cute men who carry a badge."

Either he didn't notice me saying it or didn't care. He was too busy staring over my shoulder, off into the distance outside the window. "It does seem like too many coincidences at once, doesn't it?"

"But Moira didn't have an accident."

"What if those accidents weren't accidents?"

"How many men do you see walking around salons?"

"As I've never been to one…"

I grinned. "My point exactly."

The sympathy with which he looked at me didn't exactly inspire confidence. "Are you sure you just don't want to connect the dots and see that women who date this man tend to meet with various accidents that aren't any fault of his? To prove he's innocent?"

"Listen up." I leaned in, fixing him with my sternest stare. I wanted to make sure there was no room for doubt on this. "If you think I'm doing this as a way to convince my mother that he's an okay, swell sort of guy, you are completely off base. Sure, for her sake, I would like for him to be innocent of all sorts of things, but if he hasn't? Heck, if he is a jinx, if such things exist? I don't want him anywhere near her. Things tend to happen to people who are involved with him. I would they rather not happen to my mother. Got it?"

"Got it." And he did. If it was possible for a person to stand down when they weren't even standing, he did it just then. His shoulders lowered, his jaw loosened.

Only to tighten right back up when the bell above the front door chimed. He could see the door over my shoulder, while I had to turn my head. It was reflex. So many years of working in the café left me unable to hear the chiming of a bell without turning around or looking up.

Just why Joe's expression would've changed so quickly at the site of Breanna Schultz, yoga master, was a mystery to me. I waved, since staring was otherwise very rude, and noticed the way her face lit up. We weren't exactly close friends, so I wasn't sure what that was all about.

Though I found out before long.

She stood next to our table, and her smile was trained entirely on Joe. Sure, he'd been to her classes while I was out of town. They knew each other a lot better now than they did when I took him to her studio.

Though that didn't explain why her fingers found his on top of the table and brushed against them, or why there was a flirtatious look on her face. Why she bit her lip.

Why he blushed.

Why my stomach dropped.

Yes. They did know each other a lot better now.

I wasn't so hungry anymore.

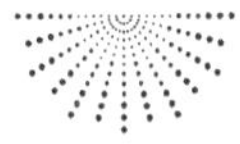

CHAPTER EIGHTEEN

"I just don't get it!"

"I don't, either. This really sucks." Raina sounded just as dejected as I felt.

"He said they've been out together three times. Three times! They had the third date!" The all-important third date we'd been teasing Mom about. Little had I known at the time how that would come back to bite me in the rear.

"You do realize that a third date doesn't really mean anything, right? We're not in high school anymore, or even college."

"Then you don't want to hear about what happened on my mom's third date," I muttered.

She groaned. "Thanks, but I wouldn't have wanted to know, anyway. Though I appreciate you making sure I got a general idea. "

Why did it hurt so much? That was what bothered me the most. Why did I care the way I did? Why had I headed straight home without barely even finishing my lunch, because I couldn't stand the sight of either of them for another minute?

Why did I feel like he'd betrayed me? He didn't owe me anything!

"I blew it," I whispered. "I totally blew this."

"Oh, honey. You didn't blow anything."

"But I did. Here I was, telling myself he wasn't ready for anything like that. I told myself that was why I kept pushing him away whenever it seemed like he was being a little too… you know. Attentive. Here I was, acting like I was doing him a big favor."

"You know what? I hate to say this, but you might be looking at this the wrong way. And I know that what I'm about to say isn't going to make you feel any better, but it might help put things into perspective." If there was one thing I could always count on Raina for, it was perspective. She was the most levelheaded person I knew.

"Well, perspective is something I sorely lack right now." If anything, I was on the verge of tears. Nobody had to tell me I had missed an opportunity. I felt it in my bones.

"Maybe he just sees you guys as good friends. Maybe your personalities are too much in conflict for anything to ever work out between you. That doesn't mean you can't be close, that you can't have a really good, solid, even intimate relationship. There are all sorts of intimacy. He told you something about himself that he hadn't told anybody else." Yes, I'd finally broken down and told my best friend what he had shared about his wife after calling her in a panic the minute I got back to my apartment.

"That's true," I whispered.

"You're clearly special to him. He goes out of his way for you all the time. You put him through the wringer sometimes, too. I know you don't mean to, but that's the way it inevitably turns out. Still, there he is. And if you ever needed him, you know he would come running."

In my head, I knew every word she said was true. Joe was a good, loyal friend. In a short period, we'd gotten to know each other pretty well. We'd been through a lot together. Heck, he'd already saved me from death once. Though Deke was partly responsible for that, too.

So sure, my intellectual side knew very well that what Raina said was logical, and more than likely the way he saw me.

My heart was another story.

"I think I was protecting myself when I thought I was protecting him," I admitted. "I didn't realize until now what he meant. I had my suspicions, but I kept telling myself it was wrong. I kept trying to shut it down before turning to anything else. Because I wanted to be fair to myself, and fair to him. What a waste of time."

"You really like him, don't you?" she whispered, her voice heavy with sympathy.

"I'm afraid I do," I admitted with tears in my voice.

"So, he's seeing Breanna? Big deal. What's she have that you don't have?"

"Should I start at the top and work my way down, or the other way around? The woman stretches her body for a living, Raina. She's super flexible, super fit, she has that insufferably sunny personality."

"He doesn't strike me as the type to go for somebody with an insufferably sunny personality," she mused. "To me, that sounds like an oil and water situation. No way could they last for very long."

"Well, there must be something he likes about her a lot, since they've had three dates."

"He probably doesn't know what he wants right now. He's still getting over some serious stuff."

"But that's the thing. Here I am, imagining this whole time that's he's been saving his heart after his wife's death. That might not have been the case at all. Just because he worked a lot didn't mean he never dated, never one time. I was telling myself what I wanted to believe."

"You know there's only one way to find out for sure, don't you?"

"Oh, yeah. Because I'm going to go up and ask him about this."

"If you're upset, why not? You guys are friends."

"Friends don't have to discuss everything, you know. Besides, every time I've ever referred to us his friends, he treated it like it was a joke."

"I think if you showed genuine interest, he would open up. What's the harm in trying?"

"Oh, let's see. I could have my heart completely stomped on. Yeah, you're right, I should do it right away."

"Or you could find out that he decided to take the plunge and figured you guys were already good friends and he didn't want to ruin anything. Or, look at it this way!" Suddenly, there was excitement in her voice. "What if he figured it would be weird, dating you while he's working with your dad? Gosh, I think that would be a pretty decent deterrent."

Jeez, the way I wanted to latch onto that. It was almost pitiful, how desperate I was to believe her. It did make sense, too, which made it even harder not to jump in feet first. "Yeah, maybe."

"I say, ask him. How are things going with Breanna? That sort of thing. Casual. I know you. You can ask and make it sound like you're just curious."

"Sure, I can lie," I tried to laugh.

"You know what I mean."

"What if he falls in love with her?" I whispered, and the fact that the very idea of it filled me with horror spoke volumes.

"You're getting ahead of yourself here. Remember what you told your mom so many times already. There's no reason to jump into anything with somebody so soon."

"Yeah, and she never listens to me, either." I snickered.

"Try taking your own advice, then. If Breanna is the first person he dated, which she very well could be, I doubt he would let himself get too involved, too quickly. Besides," she added, "maybe if you let him know you were interested, or at least not against the idea of seeing whether there's something more between you guys, it might change his mind."

"You just finished telling me he wouldn't want to date me while he's working with Dad."

"I know. Still, if there was something more on your end, it could change his mind. You know your dad wouldn't exactly be against the idea."

"Are you kidding? He would rent a tuxedo for the wedding."

"I've seen you guys together. Many times. Your chemistry is through the roof. If you were to give him a little bit of encouragement, I'm sure he would jump at the chance. You're amazing. He'd be a total idiot—"

"Please, don't tell me the sort of thing I would tell you in this situation. Not that I wouldn't mean it, because I would with all my heart, but I just can't handle it right now." And he was already an idiot. I knew that very well.

"Okay. Will you at least take my advice?"

"Yeah. I will. Maybe once this is all settled and he's not so stressed out like he is right now, I'll bring it up."

The girl couldn't leave well enough alone. "That could take a really long time, though. Who knows how things might progress with him and Breanna."

Gosh, I hated how right she was. I also hated feeling like there was a clock ticking somewhere, like I was under a deadline. "Good point. I'll make it a point to bring it up with him as soon as I can, you know, work it organically into the conversation."

"I know you'll find a way. Make sure you call me about it as soon as that happens."

"Are you kidding? I'll probably be texting you at the same time, asking what I should say next." We ended the call that way, chuckling, but I wasn't chuckling anymore once it was just me and Lola and an otherwise empty apartment.

"I think Mommy screwed this one up," I whispered, finally allowing the emotion I held back while talking to Raina to show in my voice.

A single tear rolled down my cheek, which my dog happily licked away. She was very good at things like that.

173

CHAPTER NINETEEN

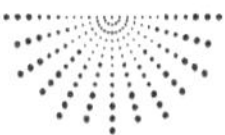

The good thing about a rainy day in a beach town was the way the weather kept people away from the ocean and persuaded them to make use of the town's businesses. Especially cute, charming little businesses like mom's café. Sweet Nothings was hopping the day after my mini heartbreak.

I refused to call it a regular heartbreak, even in the privacy of my own head, since it really wasn't anything too serious. The situation with the Landon had been serious. Very. That was an honest-to-goodness broken heart sort of situation. After all, nobody wanted to accidentally discover their boyfriend cheating on them.

When compared to that, this was nothing. I had a little bit of a crush on somebody who'd started seeing somebody else. No big deal. I could handle that. I'd handled it all through my high school years, when I was the nerdy bookworm who made a good friend but never a girlfriend. A very painful distinction.

At least for the good friend. Not so much for the girlfriend.

The presence of plenty of customers gave me something to do besides brooding—had I been home, working while rain ran down the windows, I would've been in a much worse mood than I was while handing out muffins and scones and pouring coffee.

"Are you open all year long?" one tourist asked, and she looked downright shocked when I told her we were. What, did people think the whole town shut down during the winter? Like everything ceased to exist?

Granted, I sometimes had thoughts like that. Like when I visited Disney World for the first time and wondered how they managed to stay open and keep everybody cheerful every single day of the year, not just when I was there.

Of course, I was ten years old when I thought that. Maybe I was being too critical.

Only during brief breaks in foot traffic did we get the chance to take a breather and talk about our respective dilemmas. Of course, I didn't talk much about myself. Mom did most of the talking, since I had no desire to discuss Joe with her. I'd been telling her for weeks and weeks there was nothing between us. How would it look now if I admitted I had a crush on him all along?

Truthful. It would've looked truthful. Still, I wasn't in the mood to be told she told me so—and nothing I was going through was anything close to what she was fretting over.

"I tried to call him twice last night." She looked shame-faced as she admitted this in a whisper. "I figured there's been enough time. I miss talking to him."

"You don't have to explain yourself to me," I reminded her. "I'm not going to scold you. You're the one who told him he wanted to take a little time. You're the one who knows what's best for you."

"It doesn't seem to matter," she pointed out. "I guess I really messed things up." Funny, how I was thinking the same thing about myself just last night. And this morning. And thirty seconds ago.

"You didn't mess anything up," I reminded her with an encouraging smile. "You did what you had to do. Everybody's entitled to step back and reevaluate. I'm proud of you for standing up for yourself."

"What good does it do me if I pushed him away?"

"If that was enough to push him away, you were avoiding a lot more heartache in the future. Either way, you made the right move." A new customer came in, so I put an end to the conversation in favor of turning my attention to them. Nobody wanted to hear the personal dilemmas of the people who baked their morning treats.

That is, nobody outside of people who actually lived in Cape Hope, since I knew they would've fallen all over each other for the chance to get just a little closer while feelings were being shared. They wouldn't want to miss a word, would they?

"So, you made up with Joe?" she asked in an absent sort of way, like she was trying to change the subject to something that might be a little more pleasant. The joke was on her, wasn't it?

I reminded myself for maybe the thousandth time that Joe and I had always been friends. Nothing more than that.

It wasn't fair of me to be annoyed with him or act injured when he hadn't really done anything to me at all. "Yeah, we're talking again. I let him know I don't like when he gets all Detective Joe on me. I think I deserve a little bit better than that as a friend."

"I can't believe he's seeing that yoga girl," she muttered, shaking her head.

"Breanna is nice. I like her a lot." Boy, did that stick in my throat.

"Just the same," she sniffed before going back to the kitchen for more blueberry muffins, "she's nothing compared to you."

"Yeah, but that might be what he's going for," I called out with a chuckle. Yes, that was good. Pretending to be cheerful, acting like this was something worth laughing about. And really, it wasn't the end of the world. I knew that.

But when my mother put it that way, I couldn't help but wonder what was so wrong with me. Why couldn't I be the first person he decided to date in Cape Hope? Was I too much? Did I maybe use too much snark? Were my pitiful attempts at banter a turn-off?

I kept these questions to myself. After all, she was the one who brought him up, and I wasn't about to keep talking about him. It didn't make me happy.

So naturally, what did he do? He came walking into the café not ten minutes later. Of course he did. The one person I truly did not want to see, since I felt like an idiot for having rushed away after lunch.

He looked troubled as he approached the counter. "Feeling any better?" he asked, concerned.

Oh, right. I'd given him an excuse about my stomach being upset. It wasn't really a lie, not technically, and I figured he would blame it on my unsteady state after Sangria Fest.

"Yeah, thanks," I murmured, shamefaced. "I didn't mean to run out on you like that, but—"

"No need to explain," he grinned. "We've all been there." Gee, this wasn't embarrassing at all. What would I rather have him believe? That I left in a hurry because I didn't know what the heck to do with this new information, or that I'd had an upset stomach? It seemed like I couldn't win no matter which direction I went in.

"Can I get you something?" I looked over at the sparsely stocked case. "Mom's in the back getting some more blueberry muffins together."

"I am sorely tempted," he admitted, "but that's not why I came in. I didn't even come in to ask how you were doing, though I did care."

"You're such a gentleman." I snickered, then reminded myself that I was just asking whether my snarky banter had turned him off. But if I weren't snarky, he would wonder what was wrong with me, and he'd started asking questions I didn't feel like answering. I had to pretend to be normal. Well, normal for me.

He cleared his throat, and it struck me for the first time how uncomfortable he looked. For one heart-stopping moment, I thought he might want to talk about Breanna. What in the world could I possibly say to that?

It might've been better if Breanna was the person he came in to talk about, after all. "I hate to do this here." He glanced around, noting a pair of tables currently in use. Like being in the presence of customers would make this more awkward.

"You want to go to the kitchen?" I asked, gesturing toward the open door.

He headed back without saying another word, while I checked in with our customers to make sure they didn't need anything before following him.

There was a pesky pit in my stomach when we joined Mom, who turned away from the oven and grimaced when she found Joe waiting to talk.

"This can't be good," she murmured, wiping her hands with a concerned look in my direction.

Joe grimaced, too. "I wish I could say it was, but I'm afraid not. I thought I should come in and personally let you know that we brought Bob in last night. He's been processed and is currently in a cell, waiting to see the judge."

I went to Mom, putting an arm around her waist in case she needed the extra support. "What happened?" I asked with a sinking heart. In the back of my mind, I wondered if my probing into Bob's history with women and accidents had anything to do with it.

Wouldn't it be just the way things always went? With my bragging to Joe about being a great investigator, only to have it used against Bob?

"We acquired footage of a boat sailing into the bay around four o'clock the morning Moira was found. It left minutes later. The boat was registered to Bob."

I couldn't believe it. I didn't want to believe it. "Is he on camera? Can he be seen piloting the boat?"

Joe shook his head, shifting his weight from one foot to the other like he was deeply uncomfortable. "No, it's too dark. But that, combined with the fact that they were seen together earlier in the evening and the fact that he was out of your presence prior to that, Sylvia, all points to him being our murderer. He can't explain why the boat would've been in the bay so early in the morning. Nor can he provide us with access to the boat, where we could check for DNA evidence."

"I don't understand. What do you mean, he can't provide the boat?" Mom was holding up incredibly well given the circumstances. "I didn't even know he had one."

"He swears he has no idea where it is. That it was stolen. I know," he said, holding up his hands to stop us before we could both protest. "You have to see this from our perspective. That's very convenient, isn't it? His boat is nowhere to be found, a boat which just so happened to travel in and out of the bay mere hours before Moira's body was found floating there. The odds of all of this being mere coincidence are nonexistent. And because he's not cooperating, we have no choice. We had to bring him in and book him."

Mom turned to me, her eyes darting back and forth over my face. Like she was looking for answers I couldn't possibly provide. "Am I dreaming this?" she whispered, and the note of hope in her voice just about broke my heart.

"I wish you were," I admitted, reaching out to tuck stray honey-colored strands behind her ears. I took her face in my hands. "It's going to be okay."

"How? How could I have been so blind? And here I was, trying to be supportive, and all the while—" So she had finally lost faith in him. That was how much it took for her to realize she'd made a mistake.

As for me? I had my doubts, still, but she didn't need to hear them. She was battling through enough, and my questions would only add to her confusion.

I gave her a hug, meeting Joe's steely gaze over her shoulder. He stared at me, frowning, and I couldn't help wondering if he had his doubts, too. This was police work, and he couldn't afford to let his personal feelings about it get in the way.

Still, it was possible that Bob's boat had been stolen. I didn't even know he had a boat until just now, and neither had Mom. Maybe somebody really had run off with it and used it to dump a body.

But what were the odds that the body just happened to be that of someone he had a history with? Even I knew it sounded implausible.

But there was still room for doubt, and I had to cling to that if I was going to find any answers. Mom's mind needed to be at ease, finally.

CHAPTER TWENTY

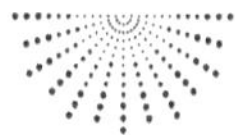

"Are you sure this is a good idea?" Joe hesitated before letting me enter the jail. I'd been back there before—there was an unfortunate incident in my youth in which my father threatened to lock me up if I didn't behave myself, and he'd gone so far as take me back to the cells to make sure I knew he wasn't kidding.

Of course, I still knew he was kidding, and I didn't suddenly behave myself. I must've been a real joy to raise.

I could only shrug. "The way I see it, I don't have much of a choice. This isn't my idea. Mom can't bring herself to see him right now, yet she also can't bring herself to stop caring about him. Guess who that leaves in the middle?"

"That seems unfair to you." He shot an apologetic look my way. "No offense. I don't want you to think I'm being disrespectful or anything."

"No, I know you care." Which naturally only made it more difficult to remind myself he was dating another woman. But friends were friends, and that was what we were, and I needed to get used to the idea.

One would think that since I'd reminded myself so many times of that very fact, it would've been easier to accept. How many times had I informed my mom and dad and aunties and anyone else who would listen that we were nothing but close friends?

"Five minutes?" he asked, looking and sounding stern. I nodded. Five minutes should be enough. I was only going in to check on him, to let him know Mom was thinking of him and that she cared very much how this turned out. She just couldn't bring herself to see him this way, and I couldn't blame her.

Even after Landon hurt me so much, I wouldn't have wanted to see him in jail.

Okay, maybe in the days immediately after our ugly breakup, but not anymore.

Joe opened the door leading from inside the station —Dad was off for the afternoon, taking Holly to a doctor appointment—to the jail cells. They weren't used very often. Sometimes a tourist would get a little too rowdy, or a fight would break out over something people from bigger cities would find completely ridiculous. Like the case of the broken picket fence Joe had dealt with in his first days on the Cape Hope police force.

Only one of the cells was currently in use, and I found Bob sitting on a metal bench with his hands hanging between his knees and his shoulders slumped. He didn't look up when he heard us approaching. He probably figured it was just another pair of police officers, nobody important.

"You have a visitor," Joe murmured. We stopped in front of the cell door, and my heart clenched at the hope in Bob's eyes when he raised his head.

That hope dimmed a little when he recognized me, but not entirely. It was a good sign, my being there. It meant somebody from Mom's life still cared, still found him worth taking the time to visit.

Joe and I exchanged a glance and I nodded slightly to tell him I was okay. He left us alone, and I knew without looking that he was waiting just on the other side of the door in case I needed him. When he wasn't being infuriating, he was being infuriatingly nice.

"Hi," I whispered when we were alone. "How are they treating you?"

"You mean, aside from accusing me of murder? They're treating me like a prince." The sarcasm in his voice was new to me, though it wasn't like I could blame him. I would hardly be in a cheerful mood if I were in his position.

"Mom sent me," I explained as if it needed explaining. "I hope you understand she—"

"I wouldn't want her here," he was quick to assure me. "I wouldn't want her to see me this way."

"She wants you to know she's thinking of you and hoping everything turns out for the best. I know it might seem sort of empty, all things considered."

"A man in my position can't afford to be a snob when it comes to having people in his corner. Believe me, it means a lot. Tell her I said thank you."

Here we were, exchanging polite words, making small talk like we'd met up at the grocery store. The clock was ticking. If I wanted answers, I had to ask my questions now.

"Bob, this doesn't look good for you."

"You think you need to tell me that?" He snorted, then looked away. "I've had nothing to think about but this."

"How did your boat end up in the bay?"

"Your guess is as good as mine. I know," he laughed, "it's a pitiful excuse, but it's the truth. I honestly have no idea. That boat's been missing from its slip for weeks. I haven't seen it since they showed me the pictures taken off that security footage."

"Then why didn't you report it stolen to the police?"

"You think I haven't asked myself that very question a million times?" He laughed softly, bitterly. "If I had only not been so stupid. I hadn't taken the boat out in ages. If anything, the expense of maintaining it without using it was getting to the point where I considered selling the darn thing. I just never got around to reporting it to the police or to the insurance company."

I had to bite my tongue. If this was true, I couldn't help but think it must be nice to have enough money that a stolen boat didn't warrant at least a call to the insurance company.

"I know very well how it looks," he assured me with another bitter laugh. "I should've known it would come back to bite me like this. Just another thing I kept putting off. It's the sort of thing Janice use to ride me over. I would put things off, tell myself I was too busy to handle them, and not until a crisis erupted would I do anything. Sort of like the story of my marriage, in a way. I kept telling myself there was nothing wrong, that I was being too demanding. It took things coming to a head for me to take action."

This wasn't what I'd come to discuss, but I couldn't help myself. "What do you mean? How did they come to a head?"

"Oh, I just couldn't bear it anymore. I found her insufferable. I guess I was bitter over so many years of being manipulated. It all came to a boiling point at once. You know, you can ignore things or rationalize them until the cows come home, but eventually, they'll come back to bite you. Just like my laziness has come back to bite me."

Could I believe anything he said? Was he just making things up at this point? There was no way of knowing.

"Well, if it's any consolation, there's plenty of room for doubt." Boy, I was becoming a real Pollyanna. Maybe I could make a career out of going from one prison to the next and cheering up the inmates.

"My lawyer tells me the same thing. But here I am, just the same." He shrugged, looking around. "I wish I understood how it came to this. You've got to believe me. I have no idea what's happening. Or who could have killed Moira and used my boat."

I couldn't help myself. Joe would kill me for this, but I had to do it. With a quick glance over my shoulder to make sure we weren't being watched through the window, I asked, "Have you considered this might've been more of a job on you than it was on Moira? This whole time, we've been looking into who could've killed her. Why would they want to kill her. Now, I have to wonder if this wasn't about you all along."

"That's just the thing. Maybe you'll believe me, maybe you won't, but I can't think of a single person who would want to hurt me like that. Who would do that? Who would put all that time and effort into setting me up?"

"Did Moira have any boyfriends that you know of? I don't think any of her friends have spoken of anyone, but maybe they just didn't know."

"Your guess is as good as mine. I hadn't even seen her in months before that night. Maybe… I don't know."

"Tell me what you're thinking," I urged.

"It had been a long time since I started trying to get a hold of those fund managers. Maybe this is all thanks to them. Maybe they wanted to silence me, and they found a way to do it through Moira. But I don't know why they would think to steal my boat. I would take a lot of planning."

"Yeah, it would." It seemed like no matter which way I looked, I faced nothing but dead ends and closed doors.

"I didn't do this. I'm guilty of a lot of things, Emma. I probably wasn't a very good husband. Being there, physically, isn't the same as being a good spouse. Just because you don't leave someone doesn't mean you're truly there with them. I'm guilty of laziness, putting things off until it's too late to do anything about them. Like reporting the boat stolen, which I could've done weeks ago. But I'm not guilty of murder. I would never. I can't even imagine doing it."

I wanted to believe him. For his sake, for Mom's sake. I wanted him to be telling the truth. I wanted all of this to be easily explained away.

There was just so much to be explained. So many

strange happenings. Coincidences. And once they started piling up, it became even more difficult to explain them away. One funny coincidence is one thing. An entire case full of them something completely different.

There was a tap against the door between the jail cells and the station. That was Joe's signal. "I'd better go," I murmured. "They only gave me a few minutes, and I think my father will be coming in soon. If he knew I was here—"

"I won't tell him," Bob assured me with a weak grin. "Thank you for taking the time."

I couldn't leave him like that. I felt my foot slipping from my mouth and there wasn't time to stop it. "Bob, if there's even a chance of you being cleared of this, I know they'll find it. And I know Mom hasn't lost faith in you. Just… try to remember that. Okay?"

It was all so empty, meaningless. I had never felt so useless in my whole life. It settled on me, dragging me down. Just the simple act of turning around and leaving him there, alone and dejected, made me feel like the worst person ever.

Joe's gaze was gentle, as was his voice when I joined him in the station. "You can't save everyone," he murmured as we walked toward the front of the station and out the doors. The sun had come out while I was inside, the clouds lifting. After a torrential downpour in the morning, it might shape up to be a beautiful day after all.

Though there was no way of knowing that, being inside the jail. There were no windows, no way of knowing whether it was day or night.

"I want to believe him," I whispered, coming to a stop at

the bottom of the stairs and turning to face Joe. "Isn't that funny? There's absolutely nothing to prove he didn't do this, but I still want to believe."

"There's nothing wrong with that. It's not funny at all, or silly or stupid or anything else you might say. I want to believe him, too. I can't tell you how hard it makes my job, wanting things to be a certain way when they're not. There are certain things we just have to accept, I guess."

Yes, like the idea of him dating Breanna.

No matter how wrong it was, I couldn't help but think of him as mine in a way. Like he was some rare discovery that I had uncovered, that only I was responsible for. How silly was that? How selfish?

This whole situation had me looking at myself through different eyes, and I wasn't sure I felt comfortable with it.

I had no idea I was going to cry until the first tears fell.

He took me by the shoulders before I could turn away and wrapped me in a tight hug that couldn't have come at a better—or worse—time.

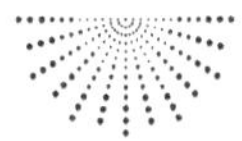

CHAPTER TWENTY-ONE

"I just thought you would want to know, since I doubt he contacted you over this. It's not exactly something a person wants to brag about."

Janice was quiet for a moment, and I could only imagine what this would do to her. But I wanted her to hear it from me, not from some gossip who would probably care more about gauging her reaction and sharing it with others than they would about her actual feelings on the situation.

"Will you be okay?" I asked her after she didn't say anything for a long time. "Do you need me to come out and see you?" I'd made this phone call knowing it might throw her into a spell or something. It was a calculated risk on my part. Again, better she hear this while at home than while she was out in public. From the way she'd made it sound, her migraines could come on very suddenly.

Her voice was weak, but it was there. "I'll be all right. You are so kind. Really, I don't think I've ever met anyone so kind and thoughtful as you. Thank you for taking the time to call me." There was a slight tremble in her voice which told me she was only waiting to get off the phone before she unleashed some pretty heavy emotions.

It would be better to wrap this up quickly, then. The last thing I wanted was to intrude on her in such a moment.

"I just want to let you know, the police are still doing everything they can. And I won't let them slack off, either, I can promise you that."

"Why does this mean so much to you?" she asked, seemingly out of nowhere.

How many times had I been asked a question like that? Normally, it was Deke or Joe asking. I gave her the same answer I would've given either of them, without the sarcasm. "I don't know. I don't want to see somebody paying for somebody else's crime, I guess. The time I've spent with Bob, I never got any feeling from him that he would be capable of this. I've been told my instincts are generally on the money, and I just don't feel that about him."

"I hope you don't mind my saying it, but that's not exactly very comforting, given the situation. You don't have a say in this."

"I wouldn't expect it to be comforting," I assured her. "No offense taken. I'm just trying to explain why this matters the way it does. And then, of course, there's my mother. She cares about him, she doesn't want him to rot in prison for something he didn't do. No one wants to believe someone they've come to care for ,even a little bit, is capable of murder. If there's a way we can help him, we'll do it."

"Bob is very fortunate to have the two of you in his life,"

she mused with warmth in her voice. "I have to say, it puts my mind at ease knowing you're on his side."

"I wish it made him feel a little better," I chuckled in spite of myself.

"I have every confidence that he'll be cleared of this," she predicted. "Like you said, I know he didn't do it. I know he doesn't have it in him."

"It's a shame none of us has much to do with the outcome of this, isn't it?"

"Yes, it is," she observed.

I got off the phone feeling lower than ever, but at least that was out of the way. I could hardly sleep all night, knowing she could find out at any time, and had barely waited until dawn to call. If her health really was as fragile as she made it out to be, there was no telling how she might've reacted if somebody broke the news to her the wrong way.

Why did I care so much about this perfect stranger?

In this instance, the reason was clear. Worrying about her gave me a way out of worrying about myself. I could admit that much, if only in my head.

I'd already been hard at work with Mom and Darcy both since before dawn; the previous day's high volume had left us short on just about everything. "Good thing I hired help," Darcy muttered for Mom's benefit as I stepped back into the kitchen.

"What's that mean?" Mom asked, innocent as always.

"It means I should be at my own shop," my sister replied, rolling her eyes in my direction.

"I think she's trying to tell you to hire help," I sang softly, tunelessly.

"Maybe I should," Mom admitted.

I almost hit the floor. That was the last thing I'd expected to hear. Judging by Darcy's expression, she was just as surprised. "You mean that?" I asked, tentative. We'd only been trying to get her to back off a little and stop micromanaging long enough to hire assistants for years. I couldn't even remember how long it had been.

Heck, even Dad used to try to convince her.

"Sure." She shrugged, looking back and forth. "It's time for things to change around here. Don't tell me you don't agree."

"I wouldn't dream of it," I smiled.

"Neither would I. I might throw a party," Darcy suggested.

"With a marching band?" I asked.

"And a drum line. I love a drum line."

"Guys breathing fire."

"Clowns?"

"I hate clowns," I whispered with a shudder.

"Okay," Darcy agreed. "No clowns."

"Are the two of you finished?" Mom asked with a sigh. "I could leave the room and let you keep making jokes at my expense."

"We're not joking at your expense," I laughed. "Come on. We're happy! We're so glad you're even considering letting some of the weight off your shoulders."

"Honestly. What's the point of having worked your fingers to the bone if you can't take a day off every now and then?" Darcy tossed a blueberry into the air and caught it in her mouth. "I'm super glad. You should've done it years ago."

"I haven't done anything yet," Mom reminded her before turning to me. "And I'd appreciate you keeping word of it to yourself for now."

"Who? Me?" I pointed to myself in mock horror. "You know you can trust me with anything! I'll only tell Mrs. Merriweather. And Nell. And Trixie."

"Enough," Mom sighed as she left the kitchen to get things ready in the café. "Point taken."

"It's a shame she has such a bad memory," Darcy snickered as she untied her apron. "You know she'll forget this the second something comes up for either of us."

"I fully expect it."

"I should go next door. It's one thing to have help but another to trust a couple of high school kids to run my store on their own." She paused, though, looking me over. "You okay, by the way?"

"Me?" I shrugged. "Fine. Why do you ask?"

"You look tired."

"You look old," I countered.

"Do not."

"Maybe not, but how do you like it?"

"I wasn't making a comment on your looks, my dear sister. I was speaking out of concern. Have you slept in days?"

"Of course." I looked back at Lola, chilling on her bed in the corner. "Right? Tell her. Go ahead."

"What would you do without a dog you could use to

change the subject?" she mused before shaking her head, leaving through the back door.

Sometimes it disgusted me, how easy it was to see through my motives. She was my sister, though, and she knew me better than just about anybody. She'd been acting like a snotty, know-it-all big sister my entire life.

"Emma? You have a visitor out here." Mom's voice didn't carry the normal knowing, suggestive ring it normally did when Joe came to visit. I guessed the combination of him arresting her would-be boyfriend and dating a girl who wasn't me had soured her a little.

Joe was busy with a blueberry muffin when I joined him. "Good morning," I yawned.

"I'm glad to know my presence bores you," he mumbled over a mouthful of food.

"You don't bore me. You exhaust me." I glanced over toward Mom, who was shaking her head as she turned on the coffee machines. She'd probably scold me for being snarky, but what difference did it make? He wasn't mine. He wouldn't be mine. Why butter him up?

"I guess I won't tell you what I came to say, then." He polished off the last of the muffin, which he must've eaten in maybe four bites.

"What is it?"

"You're exhausted. I'll be on my way now." He turned away with a smirk. I knew I shouldn't play into his little joke, but I ducked around him and stood in front of the door anyway.

"Talk, Sullivan," I warned. "Or that'll be the last blueberry muffin you ever eat."

"You're not the only bakery in the world."

"You can't chew if you don't have any teeth." I held up a fist.

"Strong point. Okay." He sat at a table by the window. "We finally got information from the fund managers."

"Wow. What took them so long? Were they all on vacation?" I sat across from him, my heart pounding. "What did you find?"

"A poorly managed office, I'm afraid." He rubbed his temples. "The mailings didn't go out because they were outsourced to a third party that didn't get the mailings processed. It's as simple as that. Otherwise, everything looks to be on the up and up. We handed everything over to forensic accountants, but I'm not holding out much hope. Besides, it still wouldn't prove anything if there was shady business going on."

"I can't believe I'm so disappointed to hear that," I sighed.

"I know. I really do. I hoped... well, it doesn't matter what I hoped. We've reached another dead end."

We wore similar expressions of disappointment, frustration. Fatigue. Like a pair of army buddies in the trenches who'd seen more than they could handle. "It seems like that's all there is with this case. One dead end after another. I don't know how you manage to put one foot in front of the other."

"You just do. That's all there is to it." He smiled, though, as he stood. "Promise you won't break into the sangria because of this."

"You don't break into sangria," I sniffed. "It requires preparation."

"I wouldn't know. What even is it?" He didn't wait around to find out, grinning as he left. At least he'd go to work with a smile on his face.

I then told myself in no uncertain terms to stop thinking of Breanna, and how she might've already put a smile on his face that morning. I was becoming old and perverse well before my time.

Raina wouldn't be thrilled to know I hadn't broached the topic of dating, but this was hardly the right situation. Besides, Mr. Hutchins was already pacing back and forth out there, waiting for us to open. Just like every morning.

Some things never changed. There was comfort in that.

Life went on.

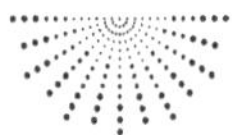

CHAPTER TWENTY-TWO

"Her? *Her?*" Trixie looked absolutely scandalized, staring over the heads of our few remaining customers to where I stood behind the counter. "*That* girl?"

Mom was sitting across from her, leaning in like she'd just dished some serious dirt. And from the disappointed, disbelieving look Trixie couldn't seem to get rid of, I had the feeling it all had to do with a certain detective and me.

She was too much.

"What about it?" I asked with a shrug while wiping down the counter. "I don't see what the big deal is. I'm sure it isn't even serious. Though if it is, it's none of my business. And none of yours, either."

"Don't be so high-handed with me, young lady," she chided. "I know the sound of a disappointed woman."

"I don't even know how to respond to that," I murmured, going back to my work. The few people scattered around the café were sipping tea and decaf, reading books they'd picked up next door. None of them were regulars, so it didn't bother me as much as it might have that Mom was discussing intimate details of my life in front of them.

But it didn't make me happy, either. Not even a little bit.

"Did she tell you she's thinking of hiring help?" I asked, smiling from ear to ear. "Isn't that exciting?"

"Emma Jane." Mom looked disappointed, if not surprised.

"What?" I asked, still smiling. "I'm just so excited about it. You deserve a little time to yourself every once in a while."

Trixie was either unaware of the underlying subtext or she just didn't care. As always, she was in her own world. "That's terrific! You deserve it! And goodness knows, Emma won't always be here to back you up. She's all ready to start traveling far and wide for work."

Hmm. Maybe she wasn't as oblivious as I thought. She both reminded Mom of how important it was not to rely on me and reminded me that I'd promised to start taking more chances and broadening my horizons. Very clever.

She knew it, too, throwing me an arch look. "Right?"

"Right." I was still smiling after all this time, though my teeth were clenched a lot harder than before. Smartypants.

"Maybe she'll find the right man someplace else," Mom mused. "In Europe, maybe. Those Italian men know a good woman when they see one."

"Why don't I just throw myself through the window to get away from this conversation?" I whispered to myself, barely refraining from saying it out loud for the sake of the customers still seated nearby.

"Or French men," Trixie added with a twinkle in her eye. "What I wouldn't give to have your youth again."

"All right," Mom warned. "Let's not put ideas in her head."

"No, no," I beamed. "No, I wanna hear more. Now that you started us on this topic, I want to hear more about these European men and how interested they'd be in me. Do you think I should take a dose of penicillin with me, just to be on the safe side?"

Trixie burst out laughing, along with the two women still reading at separate tables. I was maybe a little embarrassed at saying that sort of thing in front of them, but it drove my point home. The customers wandered out shortly after that, and we got ready to close up for the night.

It would be nice, knowing Mom had help around here. I was starting to spend more time with her than working on my articles, and there was a trip to Seattle in my near future, followed by Portland. Even though I knew my life was my own and I couldn't be responsible for her, there was no shaking guilt over leaving her alone with so much work to manage.

"Listen," I warned after Trixie had left, the two of us wiping the tables down one more time before wiping the chairs and putting them on top. "It's not fair to Breanna to spread stories about her and Joe. She's such a nice person— I've been thinking for ages now that I should try to spend time trying to get to know her better. She doesn't deserve gossip just because she's dating someone you'd like to see me with."

"I thought he had better taste, that's all." She sighed.

Watching her work was like watching an artist at their craft. She'd gotten the whole business of closing up for the night down to a science over the years. I could've blindfolded her and she probably would've gone about it like nothing was out of the ordinary.

"He's got great taste. Breanna's pretty and she runs her own business. I mean, I'd think that would at least make you feel like you two have something in common."

"I don't particularly need to have anything in common with her," she informed me. "I have more in common with you. Genes, for example."

I had to giggle. "You got me. I don't know what else to say. Just give the girl a break, huh? That's all I'm asking. I don't think she deserves to feel uncomfortable, and heaven knows I know what it feels like to have people talking about my private life in this café. It's not fun."

"Fine," she sighed.

"Has anybody ever told you how childish you sound when you're pouting?" I teased, then ducked when she swung at me with her cleaning rag.

"Sometimes I think you forget who the mother is, and who's the daughter," she grumbled, but she was in a better mood than she'd been in days, so I wasn't about to apologize.

"Who's this, now?" she asked with a scowl. "We're closing here."

"It's not technically closing time," I reminded her, though I didn't feel like staying, either. I had edits to work on, not to mention a few episodes of mindless TV to binge. It had been a trying week and I needed to numb out on something.

When I turned to see who approached, I smiled. And cringed. This was not the best timing she could've chosen. Not at all. If she'd chosen an earlier hour for her first visit, there would've been other customers to tend to.

Now, it would be just the three of us. Me, Mom, and Janice Perlman.

Well, she'd suggested she might come down and take a look at my mother, hadn't she? Granted, I hadn't expected it to be so soon. Or at all. People said things like that all the time. I couldn't begin to name all the people I'd promised to keep in touch with over the years.

But Janice was a bit more literal than that, clearly. She was all smiles as she took a tentative step into the café. "Hi, Emma!" she breathed.

"Hi, Janice." It took every ounce of my will not to turn to Mom and apologize and promise to give her at least a half-dozen grandchildren and a kidney if she needed one. I hadn't mentioned visiting Bob's ex-wife. Why would I? It didn't seem like the sort of visit to report on.

Now, this was coming at Mom out of nowhere. Never could she have imagined suddenly meeting this woman. She didn't even know Janice knew she existed, much less where she worked.

I turned slowly, trying desperately not to wince. "Mom, this is Janice Perlman. I met her recently and told her where to find your café."

She gave me a look I'd seen way too many times in my life. A look that said *Wait until we're alone, young lady*. I was fully aware I'd hear it later on and braced myself for it in advance.

She then stepped aside so Janice could see her. "Hello. Thank you so much for coming in. Can I get you something to eat or drink?" The woman was good under pressure. I had to give her that much.

"Oh, my goodness. Do you have iced tea? It's a hot one out there." Janice took a seat on the nearest chair, leaving a large tote bag on the floor at her feet. The way she was huffing and puffing, one would think she'd walked the entire way.

Just like before, she wore a flowy dress—a caftan, more like—but now her hair was pinned up in a heavy bun at the back of her head. Silver earrings hung from her ear, matching the bangles on both wrists and long necklaces resting on her chest.

She couldn't have been more different from my mother with her prim sweater sets, floral blouses, and the same powdery perfume she'd been using since before I was born.

"Have you been to see Bob? Is that what brings you here?" Boy, oh boy, was this uncomfortable. It was practically enough to make my skin crawl. I would never, ever stick my nose in other people's business again. If I had to sign a contract in blood, so be it.

She shook her head with a sad smile. "I don't know if I could see him that way, and I doubt he wants me to. He's a proud man. I know that all too well. But this is a lovely place. I'm glad he's been spending time in such a lovely place. I'm sure that once this is all over and he's cleared of all charges, he'll be happy here."

Mom's smile was awfully tight as she walked a glass of iced tea to where Janice sat. "I hope so," she offered.

Janice looked around, understanding touching her expression. "Oh, no. I came at such a late hour. You're probably closing up for the night by now." Indeed, it was almost six o'clock. I could've been on my way home, not that it would take that much time to get there. But she'd come all this way. Something told me I'd have to entertain her for a while.

Lucky me. Maybe this was what I deserved after sticking my nose in where it didn't belong. Joe would be so proud of me when I told him I'd turned over a new leaf.

"It's all right," Mom assured her. I told myself she was probably just as eager to get a look at Janice as Janice was to get a look at her. Maybe this wouldn't be such a big deal, after all. "We were just shutting things down, but that doesn't take long."

"I bet you get plenty of customers here. It's so sweet and charming." She looked around with a happy sort of sigh. "You must've put a lot of work into this. You must be proud."

"I am," Mom admitted, her chest practically puffing out from pride. "It's nice to come here every day and know I put this together. My daughters are constantly trying to tell me to take time off, but this is all I know."

"I'd want to come here every day, too." Janice stood, looking into the bakery case. "Especially with all those delicious treats baking."

At the sound of the t-word, a certain bundle of fluff came bolting out from the kitchen and spun in circles. Janice jumped, gasping in surprise.

"Sorry," I laughed, reaching into my pocket for a treat. "This is Lola. She knows that word."

"Treats?" Janice asked, and was rewarded with fresh dancing.

"She's smart. What can I say?" I crouched, petting her head.

"Can I see the kitchen?" Janice asked.

I looked at Mom, who shrugged. She wanted to show off a little, obviously—and why not? It meant proving herself as the real deal. "Sure."

I followed them back with Lola trotting at my side. To my complete and total surprise, she was growling softly as we went. "What's wrong with you?" I asked, crouching next to her once we reached the kitchen. I didn't think I'd ever heard her growl before.

She was looking at Janice as she did it, too. What the heck? One second, she was doing the treat dance, and now she was almost snarling.

"She'll have to get out of here," Janice fretted, placing her glass on the prep table. "I didn't know there would be a dog."

"What are you talking about?" Mom asked.

I looked up in time to find Janice pulling a pistol from her tote bag and aiming it at Mom. "I have my standards, ladies. I don't hurt animals. Put the dog outside, or I'll shoot your mother right this minute."

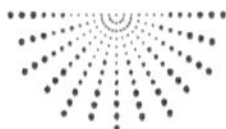

I froze solid. "Huh?" I breathed. It was the most I could do, being frozen and all.

"I said, put the dog outside. I don't want to hurt her. Or I will use this on your mother." She had Mom in her sights. "Now. And no funny business."

"I don't understand this," Mom whispered, looking back and forth. "What's happening?"

I knew what was happening. Jeez, how stupid could I be? "It was you."

"Dog. Outside. Now!" I flinched at the way she shouted. So did Lola, before she started barking like crazy.

I now knew what this woman was capable of, and there was no way I'd take a chance. "Okay, I'll put her out back. Don't hurt Mom."

"That's up to you," she muttered, glaring at my mother. "And don't even think about picking up a weapon or tool to use against me. It takes a split second to pull a trigger."

"I'll keep that in mind." It was always Janice. Here I was,

with the real murderer in front of me all along. Knowing it had to be a woman who'd messed with Bonnie's hairdryer, but never considering the so-called frail, sick Janice.

"I love you," I whispered with a lump in my throat, kissing Lola's head before opening the back door.

"Don't even think about leaving! I'll blow her head off," Janice promised, while Mom had no choice but to stay completely still.

"I won't leave," I promised as I held the door open and hugged Lola once more. When I placed her on the ground outside the door, she looked up at me in surprise. "Go. Go away. I love you. Go." I closed the door with tears rolling down my cheeks and hoped I'd see her again.

"Now. Come over here if you want your mom to live." Janice waved me over while keeping the pistol trained on Mom.

"I really don't understand any of this." Mom sounded like a woman in a trance, her voice far away.

"Lemme help you understand," I offered, keeping an eye on Janice. "Janice killed Moira. Probably because she thought Bob was dating her. This whole time, we thought it had to do with business, or with a relationship of Moira's. A boyfriend, maybe."

"You killed that woman?" Mom whispered. She was way far behind.

"I only wanted to talk to her about Bob. I knew he was seeing someone. We have some of the same friends," Janice explained, like it mattered. "I started following him around. He never noticed, the idiot. He was always wrapped up in himself. I saw them talking and it looked from where I sat like they were arguing. She stayed behind while he drove away."

"And what?" I asked. "You told her you were Bob's ex-wife and commiserated over what a jerk he is?"

"We knew each other, vaguely, so she trusted me," Janice shrugged. "I lured her to my car, promised to take her for a drink so we could catch up."

"You caused all those accidents, too. Bonnie. Elise. And your own." That was a gamble, but I was rewarded by the slight flinch she responded with.

"It was you all along?" Mom asked, aghast. Now she was catching up. "You stole the boat!"

"I knew he'd never do anything about it. And even if he did, I knew the police would have enough proof that he'd killed that woman."

"Wait a second." I was thinking a little too slowly, too, but pieces were sliding into place at last. "You thought Moira was the woman Bob was dating. Meaning it was Mom you were after all along."

"When you came to see me, I was stunned," she admitted. "I thought I'd killed his new girlfriend. Silly me. Now, I have to get rid of you both."

"But why?" Mom sighed. "Why are you doing this? Why go to all this trouble?"

Janice's eyes shone. "Have you ever been in love?"

"Yes. For many years."

"What would you do if he left you, then started dating around like you never meant anything?"

"He did!" I shouted, looking at Mom. "My dad did. His girlfriend is having a baby at the end of the year, and they even live here in the same town. How do you think that makes her feel? But she didn't go around hurting people, almost getting them killed. And then actually killing them!"

"Not that I didn't want to," Mom admitted in a soft voice. "Of course I did. I was jealous. Deeply jealous. But there's never an excuse for the sort of thing you've done."

"Oh, please," Janice scoffed. "Don't act like you're better than me."

"Are you even sick at all?" I had to ask. "Or is it all made up?"

"How dare you?" she gasped.

"You don't seem very sick to me, is all," I observed with a shrug. "You're pretty healthy. You strangled a woman and dumped her body in the bay. That's the sort of thing a healthy woman does."

"I'm sick. I'm very sick! Even right now, I'm aching and my head hurts."

"Sorry if I don't feel sorry for you, all things considered," Mom muttered, then squealed softly when Janice shoved the pistol in her direction.

My thoughts raced in all directions. How were we going to get out of this? I couldn't take any chances with Mom. If I lunged for Janice, the gun could go off and kill my mother. I'd never forgive myself. Then again, she could shoot Mom whenever she wanted.

Or not. Or she could be doing this to scare us.

No, that was dumb. She'd confessed to everything already. She had no intention of leaving us alive.

"Emma. Go into my bag and pull out the rope," she

ordered. "Or you know I'll shoot her. I've already killed to keep a woman away from Bob."

"Is he really worth this?" I had to ask as I followed her orders. "Like, what's so special about him?"

"He's my husband!"

"Ex-husband. And you didn't even fight too hard in the divorce." I held up the rope. "Here. Rope."

"Tie your mother's hands behind her back, and don't even think about making it loose and easy to get out of. I'll be checking your work."

Mom's eyes were wide, terrified. "Emma…"

"It'll be okay," I whispered, praying I was right. "Put your hands behind your back. It's all gonna be okay." Maybe it would be true if I said it enough times.

I wrapped the rope around her wrists while the pistol was still aimed at Mom. How could I get us out of this? There had to be a way. It was two against one.

Two against one and a gun, which evened the odds considerably.

When I finished, I turned to Janice. "There. I did it."

"Now, I'm going to tie you up," she announced.

"What's the point of this?" I asked, desperate to stall. If she tied me, that was it.

"There's going to be an accident here," she explained in an even, calm voice. "The oven's about to have a problem. A gas leak, or maybe a freak fire. Either way."

"No," I whispered, my heart pounding. "No way. You won't get away with this."

"Yeah, well, that's what Moira thought. And look who's

in jail for the crime?" There I was, thinking she'd be heartbroken.

Mom stood in front of me, tears streaming down her cheeks. "Not my daughter," she wept. "Not her. Please. Take me if you want."

"It's too late for that," Janice announced as she gathered up the rope for my wrists.

She'd have to put the gun down to do that, wouldn't she? Maybe I could…

She placed it on the prep table before taking my wrists in her hands, squeezing tight enough that I winced.

So many thoughts ran through my mind all at once. Adrenaline pumped through my body. It was now or never. I had to do something.

"Mom, run!" I screamed as I brought my heel down on Janice's foot as hard as I could. She cried out, knocking me forward as she reacted to the pain. She was still holding onto me and took me down with her.

"Emma!" Mom pleaded as I landed with a bone-jarring thud.

"Go! Get help!" I groaned under Janice's deceptively heavy body. I could only see Mom's feet and was glad they ran out of the kitchen, through the café. She could still open the front door if she turned around and took the handle. I'd left plenty of slack to make sure she didn't lose circulation.

All of this went through my head in a flash before Janice took a handful of my hair and jerked back. "You meddling, troublesome little nothing!" she spat.

I took her wrist in both hands, relieving the pain in my scalp, and dug my nails in until she didn't have a choice but to let go. I then bucked her off and scrambled to my knees, reaching across the table's surface for the gun. It was just inches away…

"No!" Janice threw herself against me, and the wheeled table shot forward. The gun slid across the top and fell to the floor, out of reach of both of us.

I elbowed her as hard as I could, rewarded by a grunt as I made contact with her ribs. She wasn't about to let go, though. She'd already come so far and was too obsessed.

I threw myself back then, landing on top of her and knocking the air from her lungs. She still found it in herself to hook an arm around my neck and start squeezing.

I clawed at her, flinging myself around in hopes of hurting her enough to make her let go. "No way!" she growled in my ear. "No, you're not getting away from me!"

I needed to breathe. Now. My lungs were about to burst, tears squeezing from my bulging eyes. I slapped her arm, pulling at it, but it was no use. I couldn't even lift my head enough to headbutt her, and I couldn't lean any closer to get even a tiny gasp of air.

At least they'd know who did this. Bob could be free. Joe wouldn't have to do much work. Maybe Holly's baby would be named after me…

Everything started going dark, and I realized the rattling noise in my ears was coming from me as I tried to take one more breath.

Then, like a miracle, the pressure at my throat ceased. Stars danced in front of my eyes, and I rolled onto my side. My throat was on fire, every breath complete agony. I coughed, gagged, while my lungs struggled to pull in the air they'd been without.

"Emma. Ah, Emma." Joe rolled me onto my back and held me close to him while I coughed and struggled for air. "Oh, my God."

Indeed.

CHAPTER TWENTY-FOUR

"You're sure you don't need to go to the hospital?" Joe hovered over me, frowning. I knew I was still alive, since Joe Sullivan was frowning.

"I'm fine," I whispered. It was agony, complete torture. But I was breathing, and the pain would pass.

"Emma!" Darcy fought her way into the café with Lola in her arms. "Oh, my gosh, I was so scared!"

I reached for Lola and cradled her close to my chest while Darcy hugged us both at once. "She was scratching at the back door of the shop and whining. I knew something had to be wrong, so I called Joe right away."

"Oh, baby," I smiled through my tears, which Lola generously licked away. "You saved my life. Smart girl."

I then looked up at my sister. "Smart girl."

"I can't believe you could've been killed. And Mom, too!"

"Where is she?" I whispered, looking around. The café was chock full of officers, but there was no sign of her.

"She's outside with Trixie and Nell. She got out of the

café as I was coming in and sent me to the kitchen." Joe sighed. "Not a moment too soon."

Darcy went out to get her, leaving me looking up at my savior. "Thank you."

"You don't have to thank me for anything. I only answered a call."

"You hurried."

"I did. That, I did." He crouched next to me. "I should've seen it. You told me about meeting her and about the accidents, but I didn't put it together."

"Neither did I."

"But it's my job to make those connections. Not yours. If I'd listened a little more closely when you told me what you learned instead of getting all worried about you and angry that you took yet another chance, none of this would've happened."

"No." I took the chance of touching his shoulder, and he didn't flinch away. The memory of being cradled against his chest was still fresh. It had only been fifteen minutes since it happened, after all. If I hadn't been struggling to breathe after almost being choked to death, it might've been a nice memory.

"If Janice hadn't made the choice to do what she did, it wouldn't have happened. It isn't your fault. Okay?" I held his gaze. "I mean it."

He didn't want to agree. I could tell. But he nodded, anyway.

"Emma!" Dad burst in and rushed over to me. "I came as soon as I heard. Are you all right?"

I touched a gentle hand to my throat. "Been better," I rasped. "But okay."

He hugged me gingerly. "No more investigating. Got it?"

"Got it," I whispered. I had no desire to investigate anything more challenging than my bed just then. And maybe a cup of tea.

And a cupcake.

And another cupcake. They were soft, easy to swallow.

I could rationalize anything if I put my mind to it.

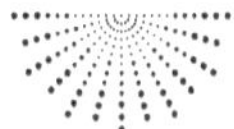

CHAPTER TWENTY-FIVE

"How's Bob doing?" Raina asked Mom while the two of them carried trays of muffins from the kitchen. I sat at one of the tables since Mom refused to let me do anything, like almost being choked to death two days ago meant I was incapable of carrying muffins.

"A lot better now that he's out of jail," Mom assured her with a bewildered smile. She was still having a hard time coming to terms with everything that happened. Especially our close call.

It was a sentiment we shared. I'd had close calls in the past, but I never would've imagined tying my mom's hands behind her back while we had a gun trained on us. There was a first time for everything.

My very wise, very discreet best friend glanced my way before asking, "Do you think you'll see him again, now that this is over and you know he's not a murderer? And you know his psycho ex-wife won't be cutting your brakes or blowing up your café?" Oh, yes. Very discreet.

"I'd like to keep seeing him," Mom announced in a soft voice, that familiar smile touching her mouth again. "He's only human, like me. He's a bit absent-minded and knows he made mistakes with his marriage, the way I did."

"Hang on." Speaking still wasn't a joy, but it was easier than it had been in the hours after my encounter with Janice's forearm. "She was definitely the guilty party. She set herself up to get hurt, just to blame it on him and get attention. Come on."

"All because she wanted to keep him with her, because she was afraid of losing him." Raina shot me a look that told me just what she thought of this method.

"I know, but still, he has his regrets. I have mine. We're both adults, both of us with a past. But our pasts make us who we are now." Mom's smile widened. "And we work well together. Very well."

I hoped she wasn't talking about what I had a sick feeling she was talking about. Raina clearly regretted starting Mom down this road, blushing and looking at the floor.

"It was nice of you to come down to visit with Emma. And to be such a big help these past two days," Mom praised Raina as she passed her on the way to the kitchen.

"It's a pleasure. Besides, you pay in sweets, and I can't think of a better salary."

"If you're not careful, you won't be able to fit into those tiny shorts of yours," I teased.

"Don't say things like that," Mom chided. "Besides, she can afford a little meat on her bones. I never knew it would be this easy to have someone besides you girls working with me."

"You know this isn't the same as hiring help," I reminded my mother. She pretended not to hear.

Raina leaned on the counter with a smile. "I'm glad she's not letting this stuff get in her way."

"She's a strong woman." She'd opened the café at the normal time the morning after the attack. When Nell asked if she was sure she wanted to do that, Mom had looked at her like she'd lost her mind. As if the mere thought of taking a day off after almost being shot was insane.

"It must run in the family," Raina winked.

"I can't tell you how much fun it is, seeing you working like a regular person."

She laughed. "It's good practice for when I help Nate run the bed and breakfast."

"I still have to get down there," I mused. The fact that she'd just made it sound like she had a future with Nate Patterson hadn't escaped me, but my throat was still too sore to pursue the topic. I had to be careful with what I chose to talk about.

"First you have your trip to Seattle and Portland, right?" I nodded. "Maybe after, then."

"Maybe," I nodded. "It'll be nice." And it would be nice to see them together. It had been a while, and they'd gotten together as an actual couple in the months since I last visited Nate's farm. I could hardly wait to tease her mercilessly over how starry-eyed she probably got while she was around him.

Lola nudged my leg, and I bent to lift her onto my lap.

"Here you go," I whispered, kissing the top of her head while giving her a treat. The poor thing would burst by the time I finished rewarding her for saving my life. If Joe had been just a little bit later…

The fact that I'd be out of town for two weeks would probably be good for her health, though I doubted Mom would refrain from shoving treats down her throat at every opportunity.

"Oh, look who it is? What could he be doing here at the café at this early hour?" Raina hustled from behind the counter to unlock the door for a certain detective who'd just crossed the street on his way toward us.

"Be cool," I pleaded.

"I was born cool." She winked before flinging the door open. "What a sight for sore eyes you are!"

"Hi to you, too." He grinned, giving her a quick hug. "How've you been?"

"I've been glad you got here so quickly and saved my best friend."

He earned a quick peck on the cheek for that one. I tried not to roll my eyes too hard. She was laying it on pretty thickly.

"I think Mrs. Harmon needs my help with the muffins," she announced before sashaying back to the kitchen. I tried to catch her eye as she passed, but she wasn't about to make it that easy. She was a piece of work.

"Good morning," Joe smiled, hands thrust in his pockets. "How's the throat today?"

"Better," I whispered, touching gentle fingers to it. The bruise was gnarly, and would only look worse once the color changed to green and yellow. Good thing Raina had brought so many scarves for me to wear while traveling for work.

He sighed while pulling up a chair and patted Lola's head before sitting. "Janice will probably end up in a hospital versus a prison," he murmured with a glance toward the kitchen. "We just got word from the judge's office."

"It makes sense," I admitted. "She needs help."

His head tipped to the side. "You're unreal."

"What do you mean?"

"She almost killed you and your mother. But you're glad she's getting help."

"She needs it." I shrugged. "I can't take it personally."

His mouth opened, then closed. "I don't even know what to think about that. I have to accept you the way you are, I guess."

"Forgiving to a fault?" I asked.

"Infuriating, but capable of humbling me. How's that sound?"

I tried not to smile too hard. "What? Do you take it personally that she did what she did back there in the kitchen?"

"What do you think, Miss Harmon?"

"You're the professional, Detective Sullivan. I'm tired of solving mysteries."

"I doubt that." He chuckled as Mom and Raina came out holding trays of muffins and scones. That caught his attention. "Tell me there's blueberry in there. I think I need two this morning."

"You can have all the muffins you want," Mom promised. "It isn't every day I almost lose my daughter. Though it does happen more often than I'd like, come to think of it."

"I'm convinced she's taken years off my life," he chuckled, accepting his breakfast with a grateful smile.

"At least you're living more healthfully now—muffins aside," Mom added with a grin. "I hear you've been taking yoga lately."

I had to hand it to her. The woman knew how to drop a heavy, heavy hint without even flinching in embarrassment. That took skill.

Joe cleared his throat, his cheeks darkening. "Yeah. Well. That was a passing phase."

"Oh? You didn't like yoga?" she pressed, eyes wide and innocent.

"Mom," I warned.

"No, it's okay," he insisted. "Yoga's all right, but... I don't think I'm quite ready to make a steady practice of it. Yoga was very nice, and I hope we can still be friends, but it's better not to take things too fast. At least, not for me."

"You're a smart man." Mom grinned, her gaze darting toward me. I shook my head, menacing, even though relief practically knocked me off my chair.

"Are we actually talking about yoga?" Raina asked.

"No." Joe exhaled. "We're not. Though honestly, I could do without actual yoga, too. It's not nearly as much fun without a certain pesky person practicing with me."

We shared a private smile when he looked back at me over his shoulder.

"Emma, don't you like doing yoga?" Mom asked.

"Weren't you saying not that long ago that you wanted to practice more regularly?"

"No, Mom," I sighed, shaking my head. She was exhausting. "I think we all know I never said that."

Though if Joe wanted to practice together, I thought I might be willing to give it a shot. Just for the sake of helping a friend. Nothing more than that. He needed to practice relaxing. It was for the good of his health.

So I told myself.

Keep reading for an excerpt from the next Winnie Reed *Cape Hope Mysteries* selection.

EXCERPT: DETECTIVES AND DILEMMAS

CAPE HOPE MYSTERIES BOOK SIX

Emma's heading out for an assignment. One she's been looking forward to until a phone call derails her plans and gives her a different agenda. And with it comes a dilemma. Deke's back. Detective McHottie's been absent. And now there's a dead body in a portapotty.

Dilemmas? That's quite the understatement as Emma finds herself embroiled in the drama of a new murder and at the same time confuzzled by the absence of a heartthrob and the reappearance of another!

CHAPTER 1

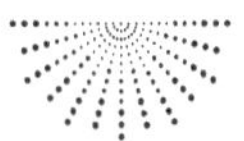

"It feels like we just got you back, and now you're going away again."

It wasn't easy to keep my cool as I turned away from the open suitcase on my bed. Not that my mother's incessant worrying made me angry, per se, but I had a weekend of work to pack for and we'd been through the same conversation roughly three hundred times.

There she was, in one of her customary twinsets, pearls at her throat. A sense of style passed down from her mother, who was more of the generation who wore things like that.

I'd always admired her for it, if anything. She'd found what she liked and made it her own in spite of changing trends. There was a hint of stubbornness behind that, I fathomed. Stubbornness she'd passed down to me, then made it her business to deride me about whenever she got the chance.

It was all very fair and it didn't annoy me at all.

Her frown, coupled with the sadness in her eyes, brought me around before I said anything that would have her threatening to put me in time out. "It's only for a weekend. I do have to work. And you have Frankie down at the café now, so you don't have to rely on me so much."

"Frankie's a godsend." That seemed to be Mom's immediate reaction every time her new assistant's name was mentioned. There was good reason for this, since the girl was a bona fide workhorse, a perfect fit alongside my workhorse of a mother.

"I know she is. Which is why I feel comfortable leaving more often. What makes me uncomfortable is having the same talk with you time and again. We both know I have to do this. We both know I'll be back just as soon as I can."

"What we both don't know is whether you'll be safe when you're out there."

Grant me strength. "It's been months since the last time I had anything even hinting at a close call, and you know it. You ought to know it. You were there."

Leaves were falling outside my bedroom window, dancing down the street. Cape Hope was preparing for all sorts of autumn festivities, the sort of thing the town relied on to keep visitors coming down in spite of the chill in the air and the ocean. It had been nearly three months since Mom and I were threatened by a gun-wielding madwoman in the kitchen of the café.

All because I'd dug a little too deep when Mom's boyfriend was accused of murder. What was the alternative? Allowing him to go to prison? I'd accidentally alerted his ex-wife to the fact that the woman she'd murdered in a fit of jealousy was not, in fact, Bob's new girlfriend.

I mean, if I'd known Janice Perlman was the killer, I wouldn't have invited her to the café. Even I knew better than to do something like that.

Mom sniffed a little, coming over to the bed to inspect my clothing choices. She'd stopped dressing me ages ago but that wouldn't stop her from speculating on whether I should bring another sweater. "You can't ask me not to worry about you when we went through that together. You've gotten yourself into scrapes before, but that was the worst of all."

I couldn't argue that. I'd come maybe a few seconds from choking to death. "It's over now," I reminded her as gently as I could. "And everything's been smooth sailing since then. I've been on seven assignments and not a single thing has gone wrong."

Which was pretty much a record for me after starting my work with Haute Cuisine, writing about exciting, delicious food in restaurants all over the country. Along the way, I'd developed a bad habit for being in the wrong place at the wrong time.

"Besides," I added, "that last little attempted murder had nothing to do with my work. You asked me yourself to help clear Bob's name."

"You would throw that in my face, wouldn't you?"

"I'd hardly call it throwing anything in your face."

"You have no idea how guilty I still feel about that." She sniffled for real this time, not in an attempt to make me feel bad.

"Don't!" I threw my arms around her. "Don't at all. Everything turned out fine. You and Bob are going strong, which is something I know more about than I ever wanted to, thanks to the way you and Nell and Trixie giggle like teenagers when you talk about him." I'd already considered sticking my fingers in my ears and singing at the top of my lungs whenever they started dishing girl talk.

"That's true," she agreed.

"And I'm perfectly healthy, no damage done. Now that you've had a near-murder in the kitchen, the café's doing more business than ever."

"I never knew how many truly morbid people there are in this town," she murmured with a scowl.

"Everything turned out just great." I patted her shoulders before turning back to my suitcase. "You worry too darn much."

"I'm a mother. It's my job to worry."

"Worry more about Darcy, then. She could use a little meddling in her life." My older sister had been in a slump for ages. The bookstore which adjoined Mom's café was all she cared about anymore. Whether that was a result of a lackluster love life or the cause of it, I couldn't say. She tended to shut up like a clam whenever I broached the subject.

Mom's scowl deepened. "She's determined to live out the rest of her days in that store, alone. We'll find her buried under a pile of books someday. Single, childless, alone."

"Wow. Talk about your high hopes."

"Don't you think it's strange? She was never like this before." It didn't come as a surprise when she pulled an extra sweater from my shelves and added it to the already overstuffed suitcase.

"You're right. I think it's very strange. But she's a grown woman who can make her own decisions. Besides," I added, shaking a finger in her face, "you can't fault her for being a workaholic. You know she gets that from you." Watching our mother build her business had instilled a solid work ethic in both of us.

"Watch that finger, young lady," she warned with a wry grin. "Between her deciding she wants to die a spinster and you, satisfied with a dog instead of a baby—"

"Hey, now," I warned. "You're the one who goes around calling Lola your grandpuppy."

As if she knew we were talking about her, Lola bounded into the room in a blur of fur and cuteness. She circled Mom's ankles before nudging with her nose. My little pup wasn't one to be subtle when she wanted attention.

"What do you think, Lola?" Mom crouched beside her, scratching her behind the ears. "Do you think your mommy needs to find a nice man and settle down so I don't have to worry so much about her?"

"Lola, do you think your grandmother needs to learn a new tune because I'm tired of hearing this one?" I chirped, which earned me a withering look.

"It's not my fault you let Joe slip through your fingers," she reminded me, picking Lola up and cuddling her.

"I did no such thing, since he was never in my fingers to begin with." I made it a point to keep my face angled away from hers when I said it, since she had that superpower all mothers had, no matter how old their kids got. She could read me like a book, finding meaning in the slightest twitch of an eyebrow.

"He could've been."

"He wasn't."

"He wanted to be."

"You don't know that," I reminded her. "Unless you two were secretly planning my future over a big plate of blueberry muffins when I wasn't aware."

"He was crazy about you, Emma Jane. Don't pretend you didn't know it."

"I honestly didn't. Besides, look where it got me." I sat on the bed, now too heartsick to continue. That was unfortunate, since I needed to be on the road soon. "He might as well have fallen off the face of the earth. Part of me wonders if Dad found something lacking in him and decided to throw a bunch of work his way to discourage him from spending time with me."

"Your father was part of the reason Joe was able to transfer to Cape Hope," Mom reminded me. The fact that she could speak of him without making a choking noise or wrinkling her nose meant she'd come a long way. I guessed Bob had a lot to do with that, and her newfound freedom thanks to hiring an assistant. Her life had opened up in a big way.

"I know, but think about it. Every time I tried to reach out to Joe, he gave me the same excuse. He was busy with work. I know he tends to get wrapped up in his cases. He takes them personally. But this is a little much even for him. What am I supposed to think?"

"That he's working hard to prove himself?" There was a

note of hope in her voice. Stubborn, insistent hope. She wasn't about to give up.

"Or that he can't think of a better reason to brush me off," I suggested, miserable.

The fact was, I had no idea how big a part of my life he'd become until he disappeared. Wasn't that always the way? Don't know what you have until it's gone and all that.

Not that I ever had him. We'd never even kissed, though we'd come close. At least, we had in my imagination. He was still grieving his wife, who'd died tragically in a hit-and-run, and it seemed respectful to give him his space.

Way to go, Emma. You let a good one get away.

"What do you think, Lola?" Mom picked up the dog, kissing the top of her head before turning my way. "Do you think your mommy should call Detective Joe and ask what the heck is going on?"

"She can call for me. He likes her a lot," I suggested.

Mom rolled her eyes as my phone rang. Then, her face lit up when she heard the buzzing from on top of my nightstand. "Wouldn't it be terrific if that was him?"

"If it was him, I'd have to wonder whether he bugged this place at some point." I snickered as I reached for the cell. "No such luck. It's my editor."

And the heavy apology in her voice the moment I greeted her spoke volumes. "Have you left home yet?" she asked, knowing I'd planned to drive up to New Hampshire to cover a new bed and breakfast.

"Not yet." Normally, I would've apologized for taking so long—not that she was the boss of my schedule, I wasn't due to interview the owners until the following morning anyway—but the way she sounded, I had the feeling she wanted the answer to be no.

"That's good, at least," she sighed. "I'm so sorry to be last-minute, though I can't help it in this case. They only just called."

"Who?"

"The owners. They can't make themselves available for you this weekend. Something about septic tank problems."

I gagged a little at the very thought. "I never want to see things like that happen, but at least it happened before I got there."

"I thought the same thing. Though it does present a challenge. We were planning on rushing that story, so it could be available for print in next month's issues." Haute Cuisine owned more magazines than I cared to count, and my stories were printed in a handful of them.

This turn of events presented a challenge for me, too, since I was counting on the money this latest piece would net. "Is there anything else I can do? I mean, I'm already packed. Granted, I packed for cool weather, but still."

All I got was a soft groan. "I wish I could say yes, but all of our other assignments are booked. And now we have an empty slot where your piece was supposed to be."

She made it sound like it was my fault, for heaven's sake. I looked at Mom, thinking fast. "There's a big food truck festival happening around here this weekend. I mean, it's an autumn festival, but the food trucks are coming in from all over the area and are expected to be the big draw. I might be able to spin something up out of that, if you think it's worth pursuing."

"Wonderful. Sounds great. The growing food truck scene, how hard the truck owners work, the types of cuisine. Terrific. I trust you."

Once I'd ended the call, I turned to Mom.

She very obviously tried to play down her relief. "Darn it. I was looking forward to having Lola for the weekend."

I hope you enjoyed *Conundrum in Cape Hope* !
For more Winnie Reed books click here!

Sign up for the newsletter to be notified of new releases.

Click on link for
Newsletter